To My Mother and Father

THE GIANT UNDER THE SNOW

A grassy mound like a gigantic hand with trees growing between the fingers, the crack of an invisible whip in the dark forest; a huge, menacing dog following a bus-load of schoolchildren back to the city – or was it, as Mr Roberts claimed, merely a reflection in the window? Who are the faceless, leathery men, thin-legged and quick as spiders? What do they want from the three children, Jonk, Bill and Arf?

It began one cold, wet December day, when Jonquil Winters left the school party to go exploring on her own in the backlands. A ridge of wet earth crumbled beneath her feet – to reveal a glinting object. It was to prove an unenviable discovery, for its possession was dangerous, and yet its loss could mean disaster. If it fell into the wrong hands . . . and the wrong hands are there, all around them, threatening, malignant, evil.

This is a fascinating, chilling story. Not a book for the nervous, not a book to pick up at night, for it cannot be put down until the terrifying climax is reached, when the giant stirs under the snow, and wakes!

John Gordon was born in Jarrow, the son of a schoolmaster. During the war he joined the navy and served in home waters and the Mediterranean until 1947, when he got a job as a reporter. He has since worked on several newspapers and is now a sub-editor with the Eastern Evening News.

Other books by John Gordon

THE GHOST ON THE HILL
THE HOUSE ON THE BRINK

Contents

1. The Hand

A cold, wet day in December. The worst kind of day for the backlands. The clouds were so low they seemed to trail their mists in the tree-tops and already, at half past three, it was dark within the forest.

Jonquil Winters left the trees and started to cross the heath. Fools, even Bill Smith. Pelting pine cones like a lot of kids. She was glad to leave them behind.

The rain had held off for a while, but now the first drops of a new shower pattered into the fern fronds. That would send them running for the bus. Too neat, was she? What was it that girl called her? Never mind! Never mind! The shoes, the 'inappropriate shoes' (she clenched her teeth at the thought of Miss Stevens' face as she said it), were wet inside and out. The pointed toe of one of them was scratched. Right! She opened her coat. Let the rest of her get wet. New coat, best dress, everything.

A copse, well clear of all the other trees, stood out on the open heath. She would walk there and back in her own time and nothing would stop her. She shook her long hair clear of her coat collar and held her face up to the rain.

The bus that had brought the school party to the backlands was hidden in the forest behind her. Its horn sounded. Time to return. Jonquil concentrated on the copse. It was neat and circular, like a little temple. She would walk round it, once, slowly, and they would have to wait until she had finished.

Bill Smith stooped over a fungus that made a skirt of fleshy frills on a dead tree.

'No wonder,' he said.

Arthur Minnett stood beside him, blond, thin and tidy.

'No wonder what?'

'No wonder fungus is poisonous.'

'Not all of it. Not mushrooms.'

Bill was a shade taller than his friend, dark, and he wore clothes that were more fashionable but looked as though, once bought, no further care was taken of them.

'You've missed the point again,' he said. 'It looks poisonous.'

'The point is,' said Arthur, 'does it kill you?'

The bus driver put his hand on the horn button again. Out on the heath its sound was thin and distant, like a foghorn at dusk when the beach was emptied. Jonquil Winters shivered. Across a sea of dead bracken the forest showed no sign of movement.

Miss Stevens was asking if anybody had seen the Winters girl. Nobody had. She turned to Mr Roberts. Her lips were pinched in.

'We should not have come here,' she said.

'Oh I don't know,' said Mr Roberts, not wanting to argue. It was he who had organized the trip. 'Even now, you know, there's something about it.'

Miss Stevens turned her back on him. He took his pipe from under his long, hooked nose. The tobacco was damp and extinguished. The wavy brim of his trilby sagged and dripped, but he could have been happy if it hadn't been for that woman. She did not respond to atmosphere.

He turned to his boys. 'Miss Stevens is worried about Jonquil Winters,' he said. 'Anybody any idea where she is?'

'Jonk Winters, sir?'

'That's what I said.'

'Better ask Bill Smith.'

They laughed. Mr Roberts' pipe stem drooped almost to his chin as he grinned.

'Well then, Smith?'

'Why should I know?' said Bill. He was angry.

Trouble enough, thought Mr Roberts, and let the matter drop.

Jonk looked around her. The copse was on a very low, flattish mound so regularly shaped it may have covered the ruins of a small building, a real temple perhaps. But four or five ridges splayed out from it like the spokes of a wheel, or the rays of a sun shape. Jonk counted them. Four straight ones and one shorter and bent. Not a wheel, more like a gigantic hand with trees thrusting up between the fingers.

If it closed on her. . . . The thought made her jerk her head up. Her hair was wet now. It hung in dark strings to her shoulders and made a spiky fringe across her forehead. Her imagination was trying to frighten her but she would not be beaten. She would circle the copse.

She stepped from the mound to one of the ridges, but her foot was too near the edge, and the rain-sodden earth began to crumble. She tried to jump and the extra pressure pushed a miniature landslide away beneath her and she fell full length between the fingers of the green hand. It seemed to clutch at her and she almost cried out, but a moment later she crawled clear unhurt.

She stood up, facing the green hand, and stooped to brush her coat. As she did so she saw something shining where the black earth had crumbled.

The horn bleated again, nagging like Miss Stevens. It was a sudden spurt of anger more than anything else that made Jonk stride into the 'V' of the grassy ridges and stoop to pick up the glinting object. But as her hand reached for it she paused. The object was like a shiny yellow ribbon, twisted in upon itself. A clutch of worms wintering under the soil? No, it was metal. She pulled a fern leaf, doubled it to make it stiff, and poked the object clear. It was circular, about the size of her palm, and was composed of metal ribbons that twisted and writhed among themselves in an endless pattern. It looked like a brooch, perhaps an old one, perhaps gold. Certainly it was a discovery; she had been right to visit the temple of trees.

She picked it up, crumbling the earth from its crevices as she turned it in her hands. There was a distinct pattern to it, and in the middle of the interwoven gilded strips was a shape like a man standing upright with his legs together and his arms outstretched. His head was a loop of metal.

Now she would go back. The green hand had given her

a gift. It no longer seemed unfriendly. Jonk smiled slightly as she bent to brush the brooch in the grass of one of the ridges. The grass was short and fine, and beneath it the earth was spongy. She pressed it and it gave. Another landslip and more treasure?

She was about to press again when the turf dimpled, as though it was going to split of its own accord and save her the trouble. But it did not crack. A ripple ran the length of the ridge, and suddenly, with a soft sound almost like a sigh from underground, it humped itself in the middle. Jonk jerked back. The movement stopped. The ridge was absolutely still. The hump in the middle was very low and may have been there all the time. Stooping may have made her giddy and she had imagined it. But she was afraid. She was able to admit to herself that she was afraid. It was time to go.

She looked towards the trees that hid the bus, trying to penetrate the darkness under the branches. There was not a glimmer of light nor a sign of movement.

And then, directly between her and the trees, perhaps fifty yards away, something showed above the ferns and crumpled bracken. It must have had its forepaws raised on a mound, but even then it was big for a dog. A solid mane of black hair made its head huge. Its sharp, black muzzle was pointed straight at her.

Jonk felt a fluttering in her throat. Breathing was difficult. Then the horn wailed and the dog turned its head. Only a dog. If she walked towards it, showing no fear, it would do her no harm. But as its head swung towards her again its muzzle wrinkled and a yellow line of teeth showed. She heard it snarl as it vanished behind the ferns, and she panicked.

Her first step took her to a fallen branch which hooked her foot and made her stumble. She landed on all fours, then tried to run before she had properly regained her feet and she blundered, half falling, through the bracken, away from the dog and away from the bus home.

A rabbit track was directly in front of her. She ran along it, able to move faster with less noise. She turned into another, listening as she ran. She could hear nothing, but the dog might be silently at her heels. She looked over her shoulder and fell flat. She put her hands over her head and brought her feet up beneath her.

The attack did not come. Gasping, eyes wide, she took her arms from her head and listened. Nothing. She stood up and her eyes searched the heath. She could see no sign of the dog. She looked towards the copse. The trees were shaking. There was no wind, but the thin top branches lashed and the trunks jerked as though some enormous thing had curled round them and was beginning to uproot them.

And somewhere close to the copse the dog howled.

Her breath hissed in her throat as she ran in a wide circle that would take her to her friends. The dog's howl lay on the heath like the gathering darkness itself and when it stopped she heard yelps as the animal came after her again.

It cast about. She could see its bushy tail from time to time, but it did not seem able to find her trail. She began to get control of herself, forcing herself to move more stealthily, keeping behind cover when she could, but the dog was making her circle wider and wider and she was no longer going towards the main belt of trees but towards a tongue of the forest that stretched out into the heath. She might be safer inside it.

She was almost there when the dog picked up the path she had used. Seconds later it saw her. She broke for the trees and was zigzagging among the trunks before it was clear of the ferns.

She stumbled, almost fell, regained her feet, and plunged on. But it was useless. Now she could hear its rush. Then suddenly, slightly to the left, and almost hidden in ivy, she saw a wall and behind it she glimpsed a roof.

It was almost magical the way she covered the ground. It was a straight run and she flew towards the wall while the dog was still weaving through the trees. She reached the wall and jumped, thrusting her hands high among the ivy leaves and kicking among them for a foothold. She got a firm grip first time, but her feet skidded on the brick. She heaved wildly, her feet found a branch, and then, quite slowly and rustling gently as it moved, the ivy came away from the wall and lowered her to the ground.

The dog, black mane bristling, jaws open and red, made its final ferocious run. She screamed as it leapt. Its jaws closed on her arm. She thrust her other hand into its mane and pulled the coarse hair with all her strength. It shook its head and the pain in her arm made her scream again.

She kicked at it and fell. She was a beast's prey. It began to back away among the trees, pulling her with it.

She whimpered. Once she got her arm around a low branch, but the pain of the jaws was too great and she let go.

She screamed for the third time.

In the ivy a door opened. A small figure came through. A woman. Two or three paces and she stopped.

Then Jonk saw her and cried out. The woman stood still.

'Please!' Jonk shrieked. 'Please!'

A growl in the dog's throat vibrated in her arm. Jonk's mouth was open as though she would scream, but no sound came. There was dead silence in the forest.

Then it happened. A crack like a whip. The jaws opened and let Jonk's arm fall as the dog was sent hurtling sideways. It twisted, biting at something she could not see. Another crack and it leapt, biting air. Crack followed crack and the dog writhed and leapt. Then it was on the ground, squirming, no fight left in it, just fear.

In the gloom of the forest Jonk could not see what was attacking it. A sound of breathing alongside her and something brushed her arm. She started back. But it was the woman. She was slim, dressed in black. She stood over Jonk but did not look at her.

In the gloom her face was no more than a pale shape with shadows for eyes. But her hands, clenched together beneath her chin, sparkled faintly as she moved them in a series of strange little thrusts. With each thrust came the crack of the whip.

The dog backed further away, clumsily, bumping into tree-trunks. The glittering hands continued to jerk.

From a long way off, deep in the forest, came a faint

whistle. Jonk turned her head. The dog was creeping away into the darkness of the trees, black disappearing into black. Then silence.

She looked up as the woman unclasped her hands and let them fall. The woman's head was tilted, listening. The whistle came again, more distant. The dog pushed through a patch of undergrowth and then there was silence again.

They remained where they were in the winter forest until Jonk, very slowly, surprised that she was not trembling, got to her feet. It was not until then that the woman turned towards her. As she put out her hands to take Jonk's, the rings that she wore glittered again. Under the hardness of the rings her hands were dry and feverishly warm. Without a word she led Jonk through the door in the wall and closed it behind them.

They walked on a path of sand. The stillness of the garden was not the stillness of the forest beyond the wall. There was a calmness that went with the orderliness of the little hedges, neat and less than knee high, that patterned the smooth sand surrounding the house. The sky had cleared and the stars hung high overhead. In the house a fire flickered.

They went inside and the woman switched on a light in the hall. She was still holding Jonk's right hand as she turned towards her and Jonk could feel the pressure of her fingers nervously altering. She was small. Even her high heels made her only slightly taller than Jonk. Her black hair was so short and smooth it fitted her head like a helmet. She had large blue eyes that moved swiftly over Jonk's face, and a small mouth on which a half-smile appeared, vanished, and appeared again. She wore a black dress and no jewellery apart from the rings.

'I could have told you the dog was loose,' she said. 'He thinks he can keep me in with it.' She grimaced at the humour of that, pushing her top lip over the lower, and then laughed. It was a wordly-wise laugh and flattering because the woman was treating Jonk as an equal, somebody who knew what she herself knew.

But the experience Jonk had just survived was being ignored. Jonk winced.

'My arm hurts,' she said.

The wrinkles of laughter vanished, the black eyebrows dipped into a frown, and under her make-up the woman's face flushed.

'Hurts?'

'Yes. Hurts.' Jonk was frowning now, angry at explaining the obvious.

'His dog . . .' the woman began, then paused as if puzzled.

'It ought to be shot!'

'Shot?'

Was the woman stupid? Her big eyes were round, simple, not understanding.

'Whose dog is it, anyway?' For an instant Jonk was in command, prepared to bully an answer from a silly, flighty little woman, but then the face she was looking into changed. The frown went, the mouth straightened, and she did not answer Jonk's question.

'I am Elizabeth Goodenough.' The voice and the eyes were steady. 'Who are you?'

'Jonquil Winters.'

'Do you know me?'

'No.' But Jonk was not certain. There seemed something familiar about the face and the black helmet of hair, something she ought to recognize.

Without saying anything more Elizabeth Goodenough led her from the hall into the room where the fire danced. Under a reading lamp Jonk's sleeve was pushed up and her arm examined. The skin was not broken but the bruises were already beginning to blacken. Elizabeth Goodenough began to massage the painful place. The room was warm but Jonk shivered. The woman waited for the trembling to cease, but it was uncontrollable. After a moment she said gently, 'Jonquil?'

'Yes?'

'What are you doing in the forest?'

Jonk found talking difficult. She had to clench her jaw after every few words to try to control the trembling but, bit by bit, she told about the school trip.

'Where are the others?' asked Elizabeth Goodenough.

'I was walking by myself.'

'On the heath?'

'Yes.'

'What did you see?'

Jonk pulled her arm away.

'I want to go home,' she said. She looked at her scratched and ruined shoes.

'Jonquil!'

It was a command to look up. The large eyes had each caught a prick of white light in the centre.

'What did you see!'

Jonk shook her wet hair clear of her collar.

'I saw a dog.' It was sweetly spoken and defiant. Miss Stevens had been sent into a cold fury by that tone. Elizabeth Goodenough smiled.

'Please,' she said.

Jonk let anger make her voice loud. 'I stood on a green hand and saw trees move when there was no wind.'

'Ah!' The jewelled hands were clasped under the chin.

I have also seen, thought Jonk, a dog whipped when I could see no whip.

Rain rattled on the window. At the bus the two teachers were organizing search parties.

Elizabeth Goodenough sat back, one hand on each arm of her chair, her feet together.

Who does she think she is, thought Jonk, a queen?

For a long time Elizabeth Goodenough stayed silent, looking at her. Jonk waited, aware that her wet coat was steaming in the heat of the fire, her mind a jumble of thoughts and fears. At length the woman spoke.

'You are a pretty girl,' she said. 'It is a shame your clothes have been spoilt. But it was your own fault. They were inappropriate.'

It might have been Miss Stevens speaking. Jonk tried to smile but the muscles of her face barely moved.

'When your friends come, you must go home and stay with them. That is where your safety lies. What you have seen today should be enough of a warning to you.'

'But what have I done? What is it all about? I don't understand anything!' Jonk was on her feet.

Elizabeth stood up, smiling.

'Some people are sensitive,' she said. 'Some imaginations fill up too quickly.'

The words had again become too much like a teacher's. Jonk cut herself off. Her hand in her coat pocket touched something bitterly cold. Very well, if the little woman was determined to keep her secrets Jonk would keep hers. She tightened her grip on the brooch and thrust it deeper into her pocket.

And then Elizabeth Goodenough's face softened. She opened her mouth to speak, but just at that moment, almost inaudible through the forest, the sound of the horn reached them and Jonk could think of nothing but getting home.

2. The Unseen Dog

As Elizabeth Goodenough and Jonk came out of the house they saw, beyond the wall of the garden, a light flicker among the branches of the trees as somebody's torch was pointed upwards for a moment.

'Quick,' said Elizabeth, and led Jonk swiftly along the sandy path to the gate. They went through. The forest was black, but Elizabeth continued to walk quickly along what seemed to be a path, and Jonk, afraid of stumbling, put her hand out so that from time to time she could touch Elizabeth's sleeve.

She heard a voice calling 'Hullo!' It sounded like Mr Roberts. Elizabeth stopped. A tiny light moved awkwardly between the trees.

'There they are!' said Jonk, and she called out.

The light stopped moving. Jonk called out again, and the voice answered.

'Is that Jonquil Winters?' It was Mr Roberts.

'Yes!'

'Thank goodness for that.'

The light now came quickly towards them guided by Jonk, and soon they were surrounded by Mr Roberts' search party. Elizabeth had been standing silently, but now she began to talk, explaining what had happened and at the same time leading them away from the house hidden in the trees behind them.

She told Mr Roberts about the dog and did not interrupt when he questioned Jonk, but when Jonk began to describe how the trees of the little copse had started to shake she gave a little laugh and said, 'All the trees are shaking now, look.'

It was true. A cold breeze was swaying the tree-tops against the stars.

'But there wasn't any wind then,' said Jonk.

Nobody made any reply to that and she was just going to describe the hand-shaped mound when she felt Elizabeth's grip tighten. She kept quiet.

'Good girl,' said Elizabeth, putting her head close to Jonk's. 'Those who know, know; those who don't know, need never know.'

'I beg your pardon?' said Mr Roberts.

'I can see the lights of the bus,' said Elizabeth.

They stood in the beam of the headlights and examined Jonk's arm while the driver sounded the horn to bring the other search party back.

'Nasty bruises,' said Mr Roberts to Elizabeth. 'It's thanks to you it's nothing worse.'

The others pushed in to look and Jonk let them while she listened to what Mr Roberts and Elizabeth were saying.

'What did you do to drive it away?' he asked.

'It ran off when it saw me,' she said. She turned her eyes towards Jonk and smiled. The smile was like the grip on her hand. It meant: say nothing. Jonk smiled back. If

23

Elizabeth wanted a conspiracy she was willing to take part in it until she knew more.

'But a ferocious animal like that ought not to be roaming free,' said Mr Roberts. He spoke through his teeth, holding his pipe firmly in the corner of his mouth. 'If you can tell me who the owner of it is I shall see that action is taken.'

'I think I know where I can find him,' said Elizabeth.

'His name?' Mr Roberts had a pencil and paper in his hand.

'I'm afraid I don't know his name.' This time she did not look at Jonk, and Jonk remained silent.

'Where he lives then.'

'Would you mind,' said Elizabeth, 'if I don't tell you until I'm certain?'

Her hands were thrust deep in the pockets of her black coat. She was looking at the ground, her face pale in the glare of the headlights.

Bill Smith was beside Jonk.

'If you'd told me where you were going I'd have come as well,' he said.

She avoided his eyes. There was deceitfulness everywhere and she was trapped in it. 'Oh well,' was all she managed to say.

They heard the other search party, with Miss Stevens, returning.

'Look out,' said Bill. 'Here she comes.'

Miss Stevens ignored Elizabeth Goodenough.

'Well, miss, and where have you been?'

The flinty face and voice made Bill's temper flare. He stepped forward.

'A dog attacked her,' he said.

'I did not know I was addressing you, Master Smith.'

'I'm telling you. She was attacked by a dog.'

Bill had hunched his shoulders and thrust his head forward. The others watched as he glared at the teacher. Jonk stepped alongside him. Both tall, both dark, both with careless hair plastered flat with rain. Miss Stevens was in the mood to tackle them.

'I am talking to Jonquil Winters. Kindly step aside.'

'And I'm talking to you . . .'

Jonk almost shouted to drown his voice to stop the trouble getting worse, but Mr Roberts' voice cut across them both.

'Smith, be quiet!'

Bill remained where he was, but his mouth stayed shut. They could see his jaw muscles knotted hard.

'That's better,' said Mr Roberts. 'Now I will do the talking and both of you shut up.' He told Miss Stevens what had happened.

'Is she badly hurt?'

'No, not badly. Frightened more than anything.'

'Bit off more than she could chew, as usual. And caused great inconvenience to everybody else.'

Miss Stevens' little mouth was squeezed as tightly as a rosebud in her plump face.

'I'm sorry, miss,' said Jonk.

She heard Bill mumble, 'What have you got to be sorry about?' He was using his 'quiet' voice, the deep grumble that, as Mr Roberts said one day, 'is the ground rock on which your character is based, Smith – a barely understandable mystery.'

'What is that boy saying?' said Miss Stevens.

'Nothing,' said Jonk before Bill could repeat it.

'That's right, cover up for each other, you charming pair.' Miss Stevens turned her back on them and began to herd the party on board the bus.

Bill continued to growl. Jonk turned to Arthur Minnett.

'Shut him up, Arf, for goodness' sake.'

At various times Arthur had been called by them Waiter Minnett and Jester Minnett, but Arfer Minnett had stuck and been shortened to Arf. He was indifferent to what they called him. Now, in answer to Jonk, he merely smiled. It was not his way to take part in pointlessly passionate arguments.

Mr Roberts was looking for Elizabeth Goodenough.

'Have you seen her?' he asked them. 'We can't expect her to walk back through the forest alone.'

But she had gone.

'Extraordinary woman,' said Mr Roberts.

Jonk sat in the bus feeling her way again through the adventure of the last hour. Bill sat beside her thinking about what he had heard and seen – a dog that seemed from the description more like a wolf, and a little be-jewelled woman whose eyes looked at you and then looked away just when you thought she was going to tell you something. She was nervous but brave enough to walk through the forest alone. Jonk seemed pretty calm, too.

He glanced sideways at her as she began to comb her hair, but suddenly she shot forward and pressed her face to the window. Half-standing, stooping over her, he also looked out. The bus had not yet begun to move. Its windows shed a faint light on the nearest trees.

'There it is!' Jonk's voice was small.

In the blackness between the trees, a glint, a double glint, twin specks of pale light. The cruellest eyes he had ever seen.

Arf, in the seat behind, said, 'What's up?'

Several other faces peered out. The eyes blinked and looked straight at them.

'There!' said Jonk. 'The dog!'

But nobody except Bill saw it. The bus began to move as everybody was crowding to one side. Mr Roberts looked out, thought of stopping the bus, but saw nothing but empty forest.

'Reflection in the window,' he said. 'Back to your seats everybody.'

'Could have been a reflection,' Bill said to Jonk. He hoped that by seeming doubtful he would get her to give more information, but she kept her face to the window and said nothing. Bill noticed her hand on her knee holding the comb. Her knuckles were white. She was more tense than she seemed. But Jonk was watching a shadow slipping through the trees as the bus eased its way along the track.

They came to the road and the bus gathered speed. Jonk's back was still towards him.

'You can't see anything now, can you?' he asked.

'No.'

She told herself the shadow must have been caused by

the bus. He saw her grip on the comb begin to relax, but suddenly it tightened again.

'What is it?'

His head was beside hers, his voice was low. Nobody else in the bus noticed them. They looked out through the same window at the same scene, and neither spoke. The bus was running alongside an open field. Beyond the field the moon hung low. In the centre of the field, keeping pace with the speeding bus, a great black dog was running.

The bus swept into the curve of the road around a plantation. Bare branches raked the moon's face. The dog was snaking between the trunks. A high hedge blotted it out. Bill raised his head, opening his mouth to speak to Arf. Jonk dragged him down.

'No!' she said.

'Why not?'

'Just us. He wouldn't see it.'

She looked at him now, wondering how much she could tell him. He saw vacant eyes, lips that were partly open and hair combed smoothly down either side of her face, and he waited. Behind her, he caught a glimpse of a shadow that may have been the dog, but he said nothing.

After a while she put her hand in her pocket and took something out, but she kept it hidden.

'What's that?' he said.

Keeping her hand close to the seat between them she turned it over. Her palm was covered by the golden disc, but she would not let him touch it.

She began to speak, softly and quickly, as they gazed

into the interwoven gold. She told him of the green hand and the quivering ridge, the chase, the shaking trees, the ivy walls and Elizabeth Goodenough.

Mr Roberts noticed their bent heads. His pipe was drawing at last, the expedition he had arranged was over, and, in spite of the alarm, he thought it had been successful. He crossed his arms, putting his hands under his armpits, and smiled. Those two would concoct a mystery anywhere. Heaven alone knew where their imaginations would take them after today's experience.

'She knows whose dog it is,' Jonk whispered. 'I know she does because she thought I knew as well, but she won't say.'

When she had finished, Bill straightened. He listened to the purr of the engine and the rattle of something in the luggage rack. The dog, if it really had been running alongside them, was gone. He had an impulse to test everything Jonk had said.

'There's a draught round my ankles,' he said. 'Can you feel it?'

'Uh?'

He seemed to have shaken her from a dream she wanted to cling to. Slowly she grew aware of what he was trying to do. He wanted to see if she could be brought down to earth. He watched her mouth close and become sulky. She turned away from him towards the window. Hedges and walls now; they were entering the city.

'I'm sorry,' he said.

She kept her face to the window and did not answer.

They hardly spoke again until they got off the bus

and then, just as Bill was beginning to make his peace with her, Mr Roberts came up and said he would see Jonk home to explain to her parents what had happened.

Bill said he and Arf would go with her because they lived only a few doors away.

'Thank you, Smith,' said Mr Roberts, 'but I'm afraid I must face the music.'

He walked with Jonk ahead of the other two. He was nice, she thought, but talking to him was not easy. She felt shy. She could hear Bill talking to Arf and caught a few words. He was telling Arf everything.

They left the city centre and entered a road where the lights were widely spaced and the traffic was thin. She glanced back. Bill was still talking and Arf, looking straight ahead, was smiling with thin and superior disbelief. Bill frowned and spoke passionately, his own belief in Jonk's story growing stronger as he tried to convince Arf.

Suddenly, still looking back, she stopped. The others caught up but she ignored them, her eyes fixed beyond them. Mr Roberts, sucking at his pipe, waited for her to explain. Bill saw the fear in her face and turned round. He saw what she was looking at and started.

'What is it, Smith?'

Bill pointed. 'The dog!' he said.

At a corner twenty yards behind them, directly under a street light, it sat on the pavement. Its jaws were open, its tongue was hanging out, and in the black mass of its head its eyes glittered.

'What dog?' said Mr Roberts. Then he asked Jonk, 'Can

you see it?' She did not have to speak; she was shrinking back. 'Minnett, what about you?'

'There's no dog that I'm aware of,' said Arf.

'I'm glad to hear it.'

Bill turned, took Jonk's arm and began to walk ahead with her. 'Let's get home quick,' he said.

'With an imagination like yours, Smith,' said Mr Roberts, 'you ought to be writing a novel.'

But Bill and Jonk could see the dog sliding behind them, keeping its distance. They turned into their road.

'I'm coming in with you,' said Bill.

Jonk shook her head. 'No. Let Mr Roberts come in by himself.' She could only cope with one thing at a time. Taking the teacher to see her parents was enough.

They parted at her front gate.

'Good night,' she said.

'See you tomorrow,' Bill said.

They turned their heads together to look towards what only they could see. At the end of the road, only its head showing round the corner, the dog watched to see where they went.

3. The Theory

The sun was shining next morning. When Jonk came out of the house Bill and Arf were waiting for her.

'Late as usual,' said Arf.

'Last day at school before Christmas,' she said. 'Nobody cares.'

Because the coat and shoes she had worn the day before were stained she was wearing different clothes, but not school uniform. She had on her coat with the fur collar. She had also spent a long time brushing her hair and looked so unlike a schoolgirl that Arf said, 'What a wardrobe the girl has!'

If anybody else had said it she might have blushed. She looked quickly at Bill to see what he thought but his mind was elsewhere.

'Where's Jane?' he said. This was Jonk's little sister.

'I didn't want her hanging around,' she said. 'I sent her off early.'

'Good,' said Bill. Now he could get round to what was on his mind. 'What happened last night?'

'Nothing much,' she said. Then she giggled. 'Poor Mr Roberts was embarrassed. All the time he kept saying it was his fault.'

Bill's two younger brothers came through their front garden gate two doors away.

'Hang on, I'll get rid of them,' he said. He sent them off together and, keen to get to school on breaking-up day, they did not cause any trouble.

'Thank goodness for that,' said Jonk. 'They always want to know too much.'

'Ha!' said Arf.

'And what does that mean?' Her eyes darkened with anger.

'Nothing at all,' he said, but it was clear he thought they were making a mystery from nothing.

Arf, the son of two schoolteachers, lived directly opposite. Jonk and he had been at war ever since they could remember. Bill put himself between them and sawed the air with his arm, indicating a barrier which was to stop the squabble.

'What about last night!' he said, but his voice was too loud and showed his exasperation.

Jonk glared at him, then turned away and said primly, 'Nothing much. Mr Roberts just explained to my mother and father what happened.'

There was a pause. She intended to say nothing more. Bill tried conciliation.

'How's your arm?' he asked.

'Still hurts.'

This was not true, and she realized as she said it that she had spoken too quickly. Now she could not tell him that even the bruises had disappeared.

Another silence. Arf glanced sideways at Bill whose head had sunk forward and was half-hidden by the turned-up collar of his coat. Arf knew the signs. Bill was discouraged and if left to himself he would take a long time to get back among the crazy ideas which had amused Arf before Jonk came and spoiled everything.

'He has a theory,' Arf said to Jonk.

'Oh?'

Another silence. This time it was Jonk who looked sideways at Bill. His long, dark hair hung untidily over his collar. He had a heavy brow and a mouth that his enemies said was big. Brow and mouth were sullen.

'What is it, then?' she said.

For a moment it seemed he was not going to answer, but then he raised his head and deep down in his chest he mumbled something.

'What?'

'We've decided,' he said, 'to do some research.'

Arf nodded.

'What sort of research?' Jonk asked.

'Well I've got a theory.'

Arf gave a short, sharp little laugh but Bill ignored him. 'That mound,' he said to Jonk. 'The thing you stood on yesterday – was it really shaped like a hand?'

She described it again.

'Right,' he said. 'Right. Then I'm sure of it.'

He was grinning as he looked out of the corner of his eye at Arf.

'All right?' he said.

Arf shrugged.

'Come on!' said Jonk.

'That mound,' said Bill, 'was the hand of the Green Man.'

They were in the Avenues, a wide road with trees and broad verges. Jonk's attention had been entirely occupied with Bill, but now, suddenly, she turned and looked back. Bill saw her coat pull tight as she clenched her fists in her pockets. They halted. The dog stood at the corner of the Avenues, in the clear, not moving.

In his pocket Bill had a penknife. He took it out and opened the blade. It would be about as much use as a thumbnail.

'Rather unnecessary,' said Arf.

Bill's brain seized a new fact. 'You can see it then?' he said, without taking his own eyes from the dog.

'Of course.'

'Jonk, is it the same one?'

He had to turn towards her to see her nod. She was very pale.

'Let's keep moving,' said Bill.

They began to walk away, looking over their shoulders. The dog stayed where it was.

'I hope you are enjoying this game,' said Arf, 'because I can see another one.'

They jerked their heads round. There were several people walking on the pavements but no sign of a dog.

'Where?' said Bill.

'There.' Arf pointed across the road towards a woman who had a small brown dog on a lead.

'You stupid idiot!'

Bill glared into the pale blue eyes that gazed coolly at him from behind their glasses. He was beginning to speak with a fury that would crush Arf once and for all when Jonk suddenly pulled at his arm.

'Just a minute!' he said, turning on her. Then he saw her face. It was taut and thin. She nodded as though

35

willing him to look where her eyes were fixed. He obeyed.

Close to the black dog, and cut off at the waist by a garden hedge, a man was looking at them. A great heavy head rested on shoulders that sloped out and down to the round bulk of his body. He wore grey, and the flesh of his face and the bald dome of his head were dull. The breath of the dog fumed about its head, but there was no sign of life in the man. His mouth was a straight line between heavy jowls. and the eyes that were turned towards them were like dark sockets cut in rock.

Nothing happened for a long time. There was not the slightest movement in the man's face, not even when, at last, he turned and, as smoothly as if moved by machinery, slid up the side road and was hidden by houses and trees. An instant later the dog followed him.

'Who was that?' said Arf. 'Humpty Dumpty?' He was angry with the other two for making a man and his dog seem sinister. They stood still until he began to move off and then they came with him, saying nothing and moving stiffly as though everything surrounding them had suddenly changed and they were wandering in a strange city. Their attitude was having an effect on Arf but he fought to make things normal again. People were passing them, cars were going by. Nothing of any consequence had happened.

'We're going to be late,' he said.

He speeded them up until they were almost running. At last Bill said something.

He spoke to Jonk. 'Who do you think he was?' he asked her.

'The one Elizabeth Goodenough mentioned,' she said.

'The one who owns the dog and is trying to frighten her.' She was panting and some colour had come back into her cheeks.

'He'd scare anybody, that one,' Bill said.

'Ha!' said Arf.

They turned off the Avenues and the school gates were in sight. Bill stopped.

'You trying to pretend you weren't scared?' he said to Arf.

'No pretence about it,' said Arf. 'Were you?'

Bill would not admit it. He set his jaw and walked on and nothing more was said about his theory nor what they had seen until, at lunch-time, Jonk worked to bring him round. Arf, eating neatly and quickly, watched her do it and was amused.

'I've always liked your ideas,' she said to Bill.

Her flattery was too blatant. He mumbled something she could not hear.

'You'll love his latest,' said Arf. 'It's his best.'

'He's got ten times your imagination, anyway!' she said.

'He has indeed,' said Arf.

She began to reply, but Bill interrupted.

'Give over, Jonk,' he said.

'Well it's true!' Her eyes were wide.

Arf smiled acidly. There was a pause, then Jonk asked outright, 'Tell me about the Green Man.'

They had finished eating. Bill stood up.

'Come with me,' he said.

They went with him out of the dining hall.

'Library,' he said, and as they walked along the corridor he spoke to Jonk. 'That mound you stood on. The hand. It reminded me of a book I was reading just a little while back.'

Arf thought of pointing out that incidents always were reminding Bill of something he had just read, but he did not interrupt.

'I'm not saying it's true, mind,' said Bill.

Arf yielded to temptation. 'Oh no?' he said.

'Shut up, Arf,' said Jonk. 'You're getting on my nerves.'

'This book,' said Bill, 'is about myths and legends, and there was one story in it that was something to do with East Anglia and it fits what has happened in a sort of way. But I mean this thing happened a long while ago when the city and everything was just like the backlands is now, so, well, the connection can't be very strong really.'

That's never stopped you yet, thought Arf.

'But it's interesting anyway,' Bill continued. He fished in his pocket until he found a little piece of paper. Jonk looked at it eagerly, but Arf knew what was going to happen. Bill rolled the paper into a tiny tube and played with it as he spoke. It was a sign he was launched.

'You know those big figures of men and horses cut in hillsides,' he said. 'You sometimes see them from the train.'

'Yes,' she said. 'But there aren't any round here, are there?'

'No. Not now, anyway. What I mean is miles away – Wiltshire, isn't it?'

Arf knew it was Wiltshire, but all he did was shrug.

They were at the door of the library. 'I'll show you the book,' said Bill. 'It tells you all about these huge men cut into the chalk.'

'He thinks one of them got up and walked,' said Arf.

Bill spoke his next three words with emphasis. 'This book says,' he said, 'that there is a folk tale about one of these huge men that vanished from its hill. They called it the Green Man, and it was supposed to have got up in a storm and walked about crushing people until it was driven out of the county by magic. Then it wandered about all over England until it disappeared into "the forests of the East". That's all.'

'That's all,' said Arf. 'He just thinks you've found this Green Man and that he's begun to twitch ready to walk again.'

'I didn't say that,' said Bill.

But Arf quoted Mr Roberts at him. 'There you go again, Smith, running ahead of the evidence.'

They entered the library.

'All I'm saying,' said Bill, 'is that some bits of the story fit.'

The library was empty. He found the book and put it on a table. They sat down.

'There's too much to read now,' he said, 'but I can tell you what it's about.'

'Be brief,' said Arf. He took the book and began to leaf through it, looking at the illustrations.

Bill spoke only to Jonk. 'You know how myths and legends, even though they sound impossible, often turn out to have been true.'

'No,' said Arf.

'There's always something true in them. Like Troy. This book says there was a German who really believed all the stories about Troy. All about the battles and the kings who were buried with their treasure, and went there to see what he could find.'

'And found the wooden horse, I suppose.'

'Oh let him tell it, Arf,' said Jonk.

'No, he didn't find the wooden horse, but he did find treasure just where the legend said it was. Well it often turns out like that, and there was an archaeologist who thought he'd take the Green Man legend seriously so he went to this hill in Wiltshire where it was supposed to have been and he did find something when he started to dig. There had been a big figure of a man cut into the chalk, but it had got overgrown and parts of it had washed away.'

'Walked away, you mean,' said Arf.

Bill took the book from him and glanced through the story as he went on. 'The legend said it walked. Well, that isn't true, can't be, but what the man who investigated it did was to look up the weather records as far as he could and he did find there had been a terrific storm just about that time and somebody had written about "water spouts that stalked the land". Giant's legs, see?'

He seemed to think he had proved everything. His head jutted forward, half a grin on his face, waiting for Jonk to be as excited as he was. She was embarrassed. It did not seem much to get excited about. She looked at Arf, but this time he said nothing. He took the book back and continued to study the pictures.

'But this all took place a long way from the backlands,

didn't it?' she asked. Neither she nor Bill had any sense of geography.

'Oh yes,' he said. 'Miles.' This seemed to satisfy him, as though by making the story impossible he had somehow made it more convincing. 'The legend says the Green Man went from Wiltshire into the next county.'

'Berkshire,' said Arf.

'Yes, Berkshire, and in Berkshire there is a similar legend, and in the next county to that there is another one. The archaeologist traced the story from county to county and they all agree about the route the Green Man took, more or less, and it comes straight towards us.' He leant over the table and as he continued speaking his voice got deeper.

Jonk shivered. 'Somebody walked over my grave,' she said.

'They say,' said Bill, 'that a place had been prepared for the Green Man here, in the city, but he never ended his journey.'

Jonk looked down at the table. 'Do you believe it?' she asked.

'Yes,' he said.

She looked up as Arf, leaning back in his chair and speaking like a schoolmaster, said, 'You are saying you believe in magic.'

Bill had both hands pressed on the table in front of him. 'Listen,' he said. 'All I'm saying is that suppose something big happened in Wiltshire, suppose a king or somebody destroyed the Green Man on its hill and claimed that now he had its power, and suppose he marched across the country pursued by the tribes that made the

41

Green Man and there were battles, well, that might have started the legend, mightn't it? All I'm trying to get into your head is that the march might have ended in the backlands.'

Jonk could see the pieces fitting together. 'And whoever won the last battle,' she said, 'might have made a new Green Man on the heath.'

'That's it.'

She and Bill were pleased with each other. They had a theory that even Arf should be able to see fitted the evidence. But there was more to it than that and as they looked at each other it dawned on them what it was – they were beginning, both of them, to believe more than they were saying to Arf. Their eyes dropped and they tried to see if Arf guessed, but he was engrossed in the book.

'I think,' said Bill, and his voice was so low Jonk thought he did not want Arf to join in, 'I think that woman who rescued you knows all about the Green Man, and something is happening out there.'

'What sort of thing?' She kept her eyes fixed on the table.

'I don't know, but we ought to go and have a look.'

She was afraid. In her mind Elizabeth Goodenough, the black dog and the grey man with the head of a statue all came together in a hideous jumble. She wanted nothing more to do with them.

Arf looked up.

'You said you were going to do some research,' he said. 'You don't call reading one book research, do you?'

'No. That's why I said we've got to go to the back-lands.'

'There's a lot more we could do before we go.'

It was help Jonk did not expect. She willed Arf to go on putting difficulties in the way to prevent them going to the backlands.

'Obviously the next thing to do,' said Arf, 'is to see what we can find out from the museum.'

'He's right,' she said. 'Arf's right.'

'O.K.,' said Bill, surprised to hear them agree, 'we'll go today.'

4. Shadow in the Gallery

Darkness had fallen when they put the school behind them. It was easy, on the last day of term, to get out before classes ended. They met at the gate. Every room in the building was lit and they could see people moving about under the streamers in the classrooms. In the hall, coloured lights were winking on the Christmas tree. It was as though they were running away from a great house in which a ball was taking place. But they needed secrecy.

Bill and Arf were on each side of Jonk, who pulled up her fur collar and buried her nose in it. They hurried, not sure what time the museum closed.

They thought of the dog, and shadows made them bunch closer. At blind corners they crossed the road to get a better view. Bushes humped in dark gardens were like the bald dome of the stone-faced man they had seen that morning.

They were glad when they were among traffic near the centre of the city. Jonk opened her fur collar as though the glittering Christmas chandeliers strung overhead in Gregory Street were pouring warmth on her.

'I thought all the time we were going to see the dog,' she said.

The main museum stood on a hill in the centre of the

city and was floodlit at night. Amber light shone on it now and they could see the pillars of its portico from a distance. It lay directly ahead of them, but Bill crossed the road at the traffic lights by St Gregory's Church and began to lead them up a less busy street beside it.

'Where are you going?' said Arf. 'The museum's straight ahead.'

'We aren't going to that one,' said Bill, and pressed on.

'Hold on,' said Arf, 'you said we were.'

'No I didn't. I always said the Crescent.' This was untrue, but he knew there would have been trouble with Arf if he had mentioned earlier that he had always intended they should begin their research in the smaller museum in the Crescent. There was trouble now.

'You don't mean you're going to that heap of old junk, do you?' said Arf.

Bill merely nodded and kept on walking. But now Jonk objected.

'I don't like the Crescent,' she said.

She thought of the lonely streets they were heading for and the big old house which had been converted into a museum.

'It's the obvious place,' said Bill. 'It has lots of local stuff.'

'Local rubbish,' said Arf.

Arf's clear mind rejected the collection which, with the house which held it, had been bequeathed to the city long ago by a wealthy and eccentric man. But Bill felt drawn to it because it was odd. He took them deeper into the narrower streets, still arguing. The shops were smaller now and the decorations in the windows were less flamboyant than in the big stores they had left behind. And they had gone too far to turn back. Jonk fell silent and Arf grumbled, but less persistently.

The street sloped upwards and a biting wind blew along it. At the top, another road crossed it, and, beyond this, other streets sloped down into a quiet area that was in the very heart of the city but seemed cut off from it. The Crescent was a wide semi-circle of big houses that put its arms half-way round a public garden. The centre house in the curved row, and the biggest, was the museum.

They came over the brow of the hill and began the descent. This was Bill's territory, an almost secret place. He led them down into it. The street lights were widely spaced and pale, stretching their necks so high they seemed more intended for lighting the cornices and upper windows than the ground. Only an occasional car came by, headlight beams rising and dipping over the cobbles like ships' bowsprits.

There was nobody in sight as they entered the Crescent. They walked along it until they came to the short flight of steps leading up to the front door of the museum. At the top they looked through the glass panels of the door. The foyer was not well lit. The walls were crammed with pictures, half of them in shadow, and at the far end, flanking the doorway into the next room, two marble statues lifted graceful arms and gazed at each other with blind eyes. Between the statues they could see the glass cases of the main gallery.

46

Bill looked at Jonk. Her eyes were wide and very dark.

'All right?' he said.

She nodded and he turned the handle and pushed the door.

Only Bill did not jump as, above them, a doorbell jangled on its spring. He reached up and stopped its hideous little dance. They stood just inside the door waiting for somebody to come, but nobody did. Bill relaxed. If the curator had come out of his room he would have watched them, silently and sourly, until they left. It had happened before.

'I know the best place to try first,' he said.

He walked quickly through the foyer, making himself ignore the marble figures as he passed between them. In the main hall he threaded his way between the glass cases, his crepe soles squeaking on the polished lino and with Jonk's heels tapping rapidly to keep up with him. Half-way along the hall he turned through an open doorway on the right and they were in a small room with one tall window that looked out into blackness.

'Now what?' Arf stood in the centre of the room, waiting for something worth his while to be revealed.

Jonk was unhappy. It seemed pointless to be standing in the cold, still back room of a deserted museum in a forgotten corner of the city. But at least, she thought, Bill was taking seriously what had happened. She would try to enter into his enthusiasm. She crossed to where a stone coffin rested on wooden blocks beneath the window.

'Roman,' she said, reading the label. 'Whoever was in here may have seen the Green Man.'

47

She surprised Bill. He grinned and slapped the stone.

Tall cases lined the walls. There were fragments of pots, a sword rusted to little more than a flake of black metal, some coins.

'I don't see how this is going to help,' said Arf. He moved about impatiently, glancing at the exhibits without interest.

'If you spent a bit more time you might see something,' said Jonk.

She knew why Bill had brought them there. Every object in the room had been touched by hands in a past so distant that these few motionless scraps were all that remained. But she did not expect they would find anything to convince Arf.

But Arf found something he could understand. Some framed maps were hinged to the wall so that they could be turned like the leaves of a book.

'What about this?' he said.

He was looking at the map of the backlands showing all the known burial mounds, the sites of ancient hamlets and religious monuments.

He put his finger on the glass. 'That's where we were. There's the track. There's a burial mound away over to one side, but look at that bit of heath where Jonk was chased — not a thing.' There was an area which, apart from the dotted line of a track, was blank.

'Pleased, aren't you?' said Jonk.

'It doesn't prove anything,' said Bill, and he began to turn the frames. He found a more recent map with roads and houses marked. 'Let's see if we can find Elizabeth Goodenough's place.'

He and Jonk traced exactly the route the bus had taken along the track but the green of the forest was unbroken where the house should have been.

'All that means,' said Arf, 'is that the house has been built since the map was made.'

'But it was an old house,' said Jonk. 'It was all old, very old.' When she had walked through its strange sand garden it had been dark, but the humped shape of the building and the warm room with the wide, low fireplace made her sure nothing about it was new.

'The more we go into all this, the more there is to find out,' said Bill. 'What do we do now?'

Nobody had anything to say. The room seemed dingy and neglected. Useless.

'Isn't it quiet?' Jonk tried to speak normally but her voice was almost a whisper. 'You can't even hear any traffic.'

They listened. There was the gentle sound of their own breathing, nothing else. The silence began to press on them like a trap closing slowly.

'Let's go.' They followed Bill into the main hall. It was a very tall room with a staircase at one end leading to a gallery that ran around its walls. A row of electric lights in plain white shades hung on long cords from the high ceiling. Smaller lights shone in the gallery.

They kept close together as they walked along the gangway between the double row of exhibition cases that took up the floor space. From every wall stuffed birds gazed at them through glass. All those eyes, thought Jonk, what do they do when the lights go out? She wanted to hurry, and when Bill suddenly stopped she pushed against him.

'Just a second,' he said, 'look at this.'

He bent over a glass case.

'I can't see,' she said. 'Your shadow's in the way.'

He shifted. There were fragments of shaped stone, a few flint arrowheads, some bronze objects and, in the middle, some pieces of metal that had been placed in a row. A typed label said: 'Fragments of a bronze ceremonial belt.' The pieces were a dull reddish gold. Each one seemed complete in itself and each was the size of a large coin, circular, but made of a continuous interwoven strip.

'Look at that!' Bill's deep voice echoed in the hall.

Arf peered over their shoulders.

'Exactly the same as the thing you found, Jonk,' said Bill.

'Not exactly,' said Arf. 'They're smaller.'

'Not much,' said Bill. He turned to Jonk. 'Did you bring it?'

He knew she had. All three had been looking at it together in school. She nodded.

'Let's see it, then.'

Her hand was on it in her pocket but she did not want to take it out.

'Hurry up,' he said.

She hesitated, biting her lip. She knew that what she had was a piece of the belt, and she did not yet want to know more. Too many things were fitting into place. If she brought the pieces together something would lock tight and there would be no escape.

The lights in the side room went out. She started, and pressed back, but Bill stayed where he was.

'Quick,' he said. 'The museum's closing.'

From somewhere below, in the basement, there was a faint click. The foyer behind them went dark. Jonk turned, wanting to run out, but Bill held her wrist and pushed her hand towards the glass case.

'Don't!' she said.

He relaxed his grip but she did not snatch her hand away. It was over the glass with her fingers crooked round the glimmering ribbons of metal.

For the first time Arf was excited.

'It's the buckle!' he said. 'It completes the belt.'

A click from the basement and the gallery above them was in darkness. Only the well of the hall was lit.

'Let's tell the curator,' said Arf.

The back of Jonk's hand rested on the glass. It was directly over the belt. There was a pause. They had almost been trapped by the silence in the side room, now they were held by the completion of the belt. The certainty that something was about to happen held them still.

A final click and the last lights were gone. In the blackness Jonk's fingers tightened on the buckle until its edges bit into her hand. Bill's hand closed over hers. Together they lifted the buckle clear of the glass.

She heard him sigh. The further the buckle was from the belt the safer he felt.

'We'd better get out before the curator comes to lock up,' he whispered.

Arf's hard little laugh echoed in the hall.

'Sh!' Jonk tried to quieten him.

'Best to make a noise,' he said. 'If we creep about he'll think we are thieves.'

Outside, a street lamp showed through the glass panels of the front door. It was too far away for any of its light to reach them. They began to feel their way towards it along the edges of the exhibition cases.

Bill tried to chuckle. 'Arf's right,' he said, 'if we don't make a noise we'll frighten the poor old curator out of his skin.'

They could hear stirrings below.

The panels in the front door had a rim of frosted glass. A shadow cut into the lower edge as someone began to climb the steps from the street. Jonk felt as if she had been waiting for this to happen. The others had noticed nothing. She made them stop. The shadow came up slowly, broadened until it filled the bottom pane, and then the figure came into view. A massive head on broad sloping shoulders pressed silently towards them. They could see no face, but they knew that in the dark side of the head deep gashes of eyes were levelled in their direction.

'It's him!' Jonk was shrinking back.

Bill took control. 'The gallery,' he said. 'Quick!'

They retreated into the blackness, nudged by the corners of the showcases which seemed always to bar their way. Bill held Jonk's sleeve. His foot kicked the bottom stair.

'Arf!'

Arf had become separated from them.

'Arf!'

'Yes.' He had missed the foot of the stairs and was wandering somewhere to their left.

'Here!' said Bill.

Arf was fumbling towards them as they heard the door handle begin to turn.

'Hurry, hurry,' said Jonk. She began to back up the stairs as she felt over the banisters for Arf. His coat brushed her hand as the front door bell kicked and jangled. They saw both halves of the door swing inwards. A dog's feet rattled on the lino.

With a hideous slowness they climbed backwards as though a black tide was rising at their feet. They could hear the dog running to and fro in the foyer. The front door was out of sight but enough light came through from outside to show them the arched doorway into the hall. A shadow fell across it. They reached the top of the stairs and crouched behind the railings.

'Keep down, right down.' Bill's voice was barely audible.

They lay flat, their faces to the bars, listening to the paws. The dog was in the hall below. There was no sound from the man. None. But the well of the hall seemed full of him. It was a black, aching hole in which he was gliding. He may be anywhere. Perhaps climbing the stairs. His foot might at any second crush them. They did not breathe.

The dog stopped. There was complete silence and then, like a cruel wind creaking the door of an abandoned house, came a laugh. It gibbered in the hall, finding its way through cracks in the air to rake their hair with bony fingers and tug at their scalps. They felt themselves being drawn out of hiding by it and they clung to the bars while it swept over them.

Then suddenly the sound withdrew, sucked away to a single point below. There was a crash of breaking glass, a hasty scrabbling, the rush of dog's feet out of the hall and across the foyer, then silence.

Lights came on and they heard running feet in the basement. Arf stood up.

'We'll get blamed for this,' he said.

Bill and Jonk lay where they were, still clutching the bars.

'Let's go,' said Arf. 'Get up!'

They began to obey him, but it was too late. The curator was running across the foyer. Arf crouched.

The curator was pale-faced but businesslike. He walked from case to case until he saw the broken one. He looked in it, touched nothing, turned and moved quickly out of the hall.

'He's gone to telephone,' said Arf. 'Now's our chance.'

He had taken charge. Neither Bill nor Jonk seemed to care if they were caught by the curator. They knew they were already trapped by something else.

5. Fools in a Fog

Nothing prevented them leaving the museum. The doors stood open, and they could hear the curator in his office speaking into the telephone. They paused at the smashed showcase. Every part of the belt had gone.

Outside, they stood on the top step. The Crescent was empty. Jonk and Bill started to go down.

'Hold on,' said Arf. He was having second thoughts about leaving.

They turned and looked up at him.

'Aren't we going to wait for the police?'

'Let's get out of here,' said Bill.

There was a sound of footsteps in the museum. Arf followed as they ran across the road to where the bushes of the public garden reached over a low wall. They looked back and saw the curator framed in the doorway.

'Walk,' said Bill. 'Don't run.' The lethargy that had made his steps drag in the museum had left him.

They came to a gap in the wall and a path leading into the shrubbery.

'In here,' he said, and they turned into the shadows.

The bushes and trees seemed full of menace, but they were soon through and out the other side. As they stepped into the road they could see the top of the hill and above it the glare of the city striking up into the night sky. A car with a blue light flashing nudged its way through the traffic at the top and disappeared.

'Police,' said Arf. 'We should go back and tell them what we saw.'

'What good would that do?' said Bill.

Nobody said anything more until they had climbed from the hollow which contained the Crescent and were moving once again among lights and people.

Then Bill said, 'I didn't think we were going to get out of that.'

Jonk shook her head. Her mouth was still too dry to speak.

They walked for a while in silence and then Arf said, 'Talk about coincidences! I've never seen anything like it.'

'What coincidence?' said Bill.

'A couple of seconds after we discover we have the missing piece of that belt a thief comes and pinches it.'

Bill groaned.

'What's wrong?' Arf asked.

'Doesn't matter,' said Bill. He felt weak, unable to face an argument. If Arf wanted to believe in coincidences he would have to – for the time being. He turned to Jonk.

'Should I take the buckle?' he said.

She licked her lips. 'No,' she said. 'I found it so I have to keep it.' She paused, then added, 'But I know one thing.'

'What?'

'I wish I'd told Elizabeth Goodenough I'd found it. None of this would have happened.'

'Ha!' said Arf.

'Sneer as much as you like!' Suddenly Jonk was wild. 'Her enemy has got the belt. Now he'll come after the buckle.'

'Come now.' Arf was superior, as maddening as a teacher. 'Whoever pinched the belt doesn't even know the buckle exists.'

'Then why did that dog follow me all the way from the backlands?'

'Does the dog know you have it?' Arf's eyebrows were raised.

For a moment Jonk was speechless. Nothing would ever convince Arf.

Bill said, 'When Jonk put the buckle close to the belt something happened.'

'It certainly did,' said Arf. 'You two went off your heads.'

'If you'd had the buckle in your hand at that moment you wouldn't be talking like this now!' said Jonk.

'Really?' Arf smiled. No matter what they said, Arf smiled. They tried to argue a different expression on to his face, even half-hoping the black dog would appear again to make their fears certain, but all the way home they had no sight of it.

'There's one thing we're going to do anyway,' said Bill. 'Tomorrow we are going to see Elizabeth Good-enough.'

He knew that Jonk would agree, but Arf did not object either, although he was still trying to insist that they should tell somebody else about the theft when, at the corner of their road, they met Jonk's father on his way home from work. He was a small man with quick, suspicious eyes that always made Bill feel uncomfortable. He had already written letters to the authorities about dangerous dogs in the backlands, and when he saw them he sensed that something was wrong.

'All right, Jonquil?' he said.

'Yes, Dad.'

'No more trouble?'

'Of course not. How could there be?'

So, thought Arf, not even parents are to be told.

But when she got home both Jonk's parents guessed something was on her mind. She was subdued, content to do nothing all evening but watch television, and they noticed her eyes wander often from the screen to the Christmas tree where, through the glitter of its decorations, she gazed at the hidden branches and forgot where she was. They saw her frown from time to time and thought she was suffering from a reaction to her experience the day before. They tried to get her to go to bed before Jane, but Jonk refused to be coddled – 'and that,' she overheard her mother say, 'worries me most of all.'

In the morning there was thick fog. Bill felt shut in. His brothers were noisy and his mother was bustling about, but he sat eating his breakfast in silence.

His father came in from outside, the short black working coat he wore on the building site glistening with damp.

'Blasted fog!' he said. 'I can't get the car started.'

'Oh not again!' said Bill's mother.

'Give me a hand, will you?' he said to Bill.

Bill got his coat and went out. 'Want a push?' he said.

'No, you get in and give the accelerator a jab as soon as she fires. I'll give her a swing.'

But in the end they had to push it and at last it started. Bill stood in the road watching the car cough its way into the fog. It disappeared but he listened until he could hear it no more.

The houses on either side looked at each other blank-faced. Not a curtain stirred. The ends of the road were lost in fog. It was as though he was in a courtyard in a deserted town. He stood quite still. Behind him there was a sound so faint it could have been his own hair brushing his collar. He spun round. Only empty fog. He held his breath and the sound came again, but in front of him this time. And then, at the foot of the fog, in the gutter to his right, something slid towards him. A rat was running at the pavement's edge.

It thought it was alone and began to cross the road, obliquely, heading straight for him. He stamped his foot and its two sharp black eyes turned on him suddenly. It may have been fear that made it stop and rear up, but as it did so its little pink mouth opened and a sound like a tiny hissing snarl came from it. Then it turned and ran away.

Bill felt himself tremble. Only a rat, but it had seemed like a messenger.

'Stop,' he growled. He wanted to go indoors, run away, but he refused to let himself do it. Instead, he crossed to Arf's house and rang the bell. His mother would think that as his holiday had begun he had gone to work with his father as he sometimes did.

As both of Arf's parents were teachers the entire household was on holiday. Arf had made breakfast and taken it up to them with the papers.

'Splendid!' said his father, a tubby man who liked nothing better than breakfast in bed with something to read. He put on his glasses and reached immediately for *The Times Literary Supplement*.

'That takes care of him,' said Arf's mother. She was a small woman, chirpy, the only one whose teasing he encouraged, but even she could sometimes make him wince. She did so now. 'And here's a reward for a good little boy,' she said and threw him a colour supplement.

Arf lit the gas fire and sat on the floor in front of it. They were all still drinking tea and reading when the doorbell rang.

Bill waited in the kitchen while Arf dressed and then they crossed the road to Jonk's house. Her mother opened the door. She looked harassed.

'Jonquil!' she called. 'Somebody to see you.'

'Shan't be a minute.'

Jonk eventually came to the door dressed to go out. She was not wearing her fur collar, but the raincoat she had on was, as she had told herself, more appropriate for what lay ahead. She pulled the belt very tight around her waist.

'I've told you not to do that,' said her mother. 'It makes your coat all creased.'

'I like it,' said Jonk.

'I can see you're your old self again,' said Mrs Winters. 'I thought you were going to stay in this morning and help me.'

'I'm sorry, Mother, but I promised.'

Mrs Winters sighed. 'Well don't be late,' she said.

As they walked up the road, Jonk said, 'She thinks I'm going to buy Christmas presents.'

'Sly little devil,' said Bill.

'What about the buckle?' Arf asked.

Jonk stopped short. 'Oh, I forgot it!'

Arf looked at her sharply. She would hardly have forgotten something so important. She made as if to go back but Bill prevented her.

'We are better off without it,' he said.

Arf thought it very foolish not to take the evidence with them, but he guessed what was on their minds. They were both superstitious enough to believe that the buckle attracted danger.

The fog was very dense. On the way to the bus station they waited in shop doorways several times to see if anything was following them, but the mist had no secrets. They began to think of it as friendly, something for they themselves to hide in, but it made the bus journey slow.

There was also trouble with the conductor, as they did not know exactly where they wanted to get off.

'Tell you what I'll do,' he said. 'When we reach the place, you tell me and you can pay then.'

'If we ever recognize it,' said Arf.

Once they were outside the city the fog lifted a little and the bus made better speed. Jonk kept her face to the window trying to penetrate the greyness that lay on the fields. The far hedges were out of sight, and in the hidden distances she imagined the dog running as it had run through the night. She saw nothing but she shuddered.

After a few miles the fog thickened and the bus pushed into it slowly.

'What about this, then?' said Arf.

Bill leant across Jonk to look out. There had been no hedge where the school bus had turned off, just open country and a track. It would be hard to pick out. He recognized the edge of a plantation and then for a long time could be sure of nothing. The headlights of on-coming cars did not show their yellow discs until they were only a bus length away and even when they were alongside they did nothing to show what was at the road-side. And gradually even the hedges fell away and there was nothing to see beyond the verge but the blank face of the fog.

'Where are we now?' said Arf.

'I don't know,' Bill admitted.

'Why don't we give up and go back?'

'No!' Jonk overruled him. 'I'll tell you when we get off.'

She had her head half-turned towards the window but was making no effort to see into the fog.

Arf was sarcastic. 'Clever kid!' he said, but Bill watched Jonk closely. She was not usually good at finding her way around, but now, in the worst con-ditions, she seemed to have no doubts.

Within herself, Jonk questioned nothing. She knew she would know when they were there. Seven minutes went by before she did a thing. Then suddenly she said 'Now' and they stood up.

'Here?' said the conductor. Bill nodded, and the conductor rang the bell. 'There's nothing here, you know,' he said. 'Nothing for miles.'

'We're meeting somebody,' Bill said.

'Hope they turn up,' said the conductor.

They put up their collars as they watched the fog fold in behind the bus, and then, with Jonk leading, they crossed the road and went back a few yards.

'Spot on!' said Bill. 'How did you do it?'

'We must be mad,' said Arf. 'Some fool steals something from a museum and we end up out here. Miles from anywhere. Cut off. Three fools in a fog.'

Jonk paid no attention to what they were saying, and she herself said nothing. She led them into the mouth of the track. The damp sand deadened their footfalls, and behind them the whine of the occasional car crawling through the fog in low gear was muffled and then extinguished. They were alone.

6. The Leather Men

The fog held everything still. The trees had swallowed the birds, and the grass bowed as though it would die.

They kept to the track. When they came to the place where the school bus had waited Bill said, 'Green hand first.' He had an appetite, as Jonk had feared, for everything.

She led them through the narrow band of forest to the edge of the heath and pointed into the fog. 'Only if you think it's necessary,' she said.

Bill took the lead along the twisting rabbit tracks. The ferns were nowhere more than waist-high. It was like wading out to sea. The forest disappeared behind them, and the copse was still invisible, but Jonk's sense of direction was sure and whenever he asked her which turning to take she told him without having to hesitate.

Once, suddenly, she made him stop.

'What is it?' He kept his voice low and all three crouched, sinking into the ferns.

She pointed. To the right of them, at the limit of visibility, a shape humped in the mist. Jonk's breath was thin and quick. The shape was like the dog's black mane.

'It's just a bit of undergrowth,' said Arf.

'No, it's moving. Look!'

It seemed to change shape.

'It's the effect of the fog,' said Bill.

He led them towards it. It was a clump of ferns standing higher than the rest but, submerged in the fog, every shape seemed to hold a danger.

They pushed on until the trees of the grove appeared. The bare branches were black lines drawn on the greyness, quite still. They went closer.

'Where's this famous hand?' Arf spoke loudly, afraid of no mystery.

They went forward quickly. The green swelling ridges were splayed out among the trees.

'Doesn't look much like a hand to me,' said Arf, and kicked the turf.

'Come away!' Jonk drew back, but now Bill climbed one of the ridges and began to walk along it to the centre of the grove. Just as Jonk had done two days before, he counted the fingers. It looked, as she had said, like a great clumsy hand. He turned round. There was even a wrist. A thick, rounded hump joined the hand and stretched from it through the grove and out at the other side for as far as he could see.

'Hey, Jonk!' he called. 'I can't remember you saying anything about an arm.'

'I didn't.' She would come no closer than the tips of the fingers.

'Well it's got one. Come and look.'

She told him again to come down. 'Please,' she said, 'please.'

She badly wanted him to show some fear, but he was excited, interested in the shapes.

'Must have been made years ago,' he said. 'Thick turf

65

over everything and trees and bushes growing from it.'

'No,' she said, 'not trees.' All she wanted was for him to come down, but she had to tell him about the trees.

He looked round. 'You're right. The trees are between the fingers.'

He walked out along one of the ridges towards her and jumped off. The ridge was as high as his waist.

'What's wrong, Jonk? What are you looking at?'

Her face had gone very pale and her eyes were fixed on the ridge. She pulled him away.

'It's grown!' she said. 'Honestly. Those ridges only came up this high.' She put a hand on her knee.

He did not completely believe her, but he saw how afraid she was and he did not argue.

'All right,' he said, 'we'll go to the house now. Where's Arf?'

They could see him at the other side of the grove. When they got round to him he was examining the bank that Bill had seen from the hand.

'It really is like an arm, Jonk,' said Bill.

She licked her lips and nodded, but refused to go closer. Arf began to walk away from them alongside the bank. It was too tall to see over.

'I just want to see how long it is,' he said.

'Come back!'

Jonk almost shrieked. Arf stopped, eyebrows raised.

'What's wrong with you?'

'It wasn't there before,' she said. 'Come away, please.'

Beyond Arf, out on the heath, she knew there was

something worse. She could almost see the side of the Green Man's body raised like a cliff.

'What rubbish you talk!' said Arf. 'This is as old as the hills. It's a long burial mound or something.'

'I bet you're right,' said Bill. He took a step towards Arf but Jonk snatched at his arm, and he called out to Arf, 'It's no good exploring that now. Let's get to the house.'

Reluctantly, Arf came with them, but he looked back from time to time, even after the mound was out of sight, and he fell silent.

'What is it?' said Bill.

'Nothing.'

Bill knew better than to press him, but he too began to look back as they followed Jonk. She stopped when she could see the dark wall of the forest.

'Must get my breath,' she said.

Their breath added mist to mist. Now they had stopped moving they once more felt the silence of the heath. Then suddenly their skin seemed to shrink and their flesh go iron-hard. Behind them, in the crawling fog, came a soft, gentle sound. Something rustled, pushing towards them.

'Down!' Bill pulled at them, and they crouched.

The sound continued for a second and then stopped.

Arf pointed. He said nothing. At the edge of their vision, sunk deep in the vapour, stood the figure of a man.

They stayed where they were. The figure did not move. Something like anger brought Bill to his feet.

'Hullo!' he called. No movement. 'Hullo!'

Jonk and Arf stood up.

'Dead tree,' said Bill. 'A rotten, lousy, dead tree.' He started to walk towards it.

'Don't go!' said Jonk.

Bill went a few more paces and stopped.

'I can see it now,' he said. 'It's only a tree.'

They turned and left it behind, running now. Twice they stopped, listening for the rustling, but heard nothing. It had probably been some small animal. They slowed to a walk among the trunks of the forest.

'Oh,' said Jonk, 'that was horrible!'

She was looking ahead for the house and Bill was asking how far it was. Neither saw what Arf saw.

He was behind them. Away to his right he thought something moved behind a tree. He clenched his teeth until his jaw hurt. Had he seen anything? He was not sure. A moment later his thin mouth smiled. He had been tricked by a simple illusion. The rows of trees appeared to move as he walked among them. He turned his head to the left, looking for the same effect, and it happened again. His smile widened as he thought of how he could startle the other two. But he would let them find the house first. He paused to pick up a fir cone to throw among the branches.

He straightened, still smiling, and watched a tree away to one side move until another blotted it out. His smile tightened a little. The tree had seemed to keep moving although he himself was standing still. He had stooped; that had caused it. He was about to test it when the tree moved again. But it was not a tree. A thin figure of a man was stepping between the trunks.

The others were only just ahead of him. He opened his mouth and was surprised that no words came. He ran until he blundered into Bill, and pointed.

The man was not attempting to hide. He was level with them, just visible in the fog. Then he seemed to see them, and stopped.

'Hey!' Bill shouted, but the man, like the dead tree on the heath, remained still.

They clustered together. A faint sound made them turn their heads. Stepping on long, thin legs over fallen branches, another man came through the mist. He halted when, like the other, he was just visible. Both tall, both very thin, they stood like two carved images that had been placed among the trees.

Bill pulled Jonk's sleeve, and all three moved off slowly. Delicate long legs prodded the ground, keeping level. As fear rose they began to run. The men scuttled with them like gigantic spiders.

For Jonk a nightmare was repeating itself. She knew the panic in her lungs like an old enemy. She wanted to push her arms forwards and swim through the fog to safe sunshine, but the grey wall remained ahead of her and she ran blindly.

The nightmare was new to Bill and Arf and they ran less well, stumbling.

The figure behind them worked its way round to their left, and now they were running between the two of them as though they were being herded like cattle. But gradually the figures drew ahead, flickering between the trunks.

Arf snatched at the arms of Jonk and Bill.

'Stop!' he said. 'Make for the road!'

Jonk shook him off. 'No! No! They want to head us off!'

She could see the dark barrier of the ivy-covered wall around Elizabeth Goodenough's house. Her feet thudded in the carpet of pine needles. It was like trying to run on sponge.

The men were ahead now and drawing closer together. And then they stopped. The way to the house was cut off.

Jonk wheeled right. The man kept between them and the wall.

'Elizabeth!' Jonk called. Her voice was too thin. She stopped, gulped air, and yelled again. Bill and Arf did the same, trying to make their voices carry through the fog to the house they still could not see at the other side of the wall.

The men for the first time were not quiet. They called to each other, a harsh sound, like branches splitting, cold and vicious. And they advanced, slowly, picking their way.

The three began to fall back, shouting until the wall was lost behind a curtain of fog. They fell silent except for the breath whistling in their throats. They retreated through the trees, farther and farther from the house.

Clear and as fragile as glass, the idea sprang into Bill's mind. They had to stop or lose everything. Suddenly, without a word, he pressed both feet into the pine needles and stood still. The voices barked at him, slashing like whips. He could not stand still, yet he had told himself he would not fall back. He ran into the din.

The sounds stung. He half-closed his eyes and made for the space between the men. The noise was terrible. Only a noise, only a noise, only a noise. He threw himself into it. He lashed with his stick as though to beat it down, but it thickened. It dragged at his mind and slowed it with fear. He ran on until he heard from his own mouth a sound like a whimper. Ahead of him, as still as a tree, stood one of the men, twenty paces away. Bill swerved. The man came with him. Bill turned towards him, took one more pace, faltered and stopped.

The man thrust his head towards him, snarling. For the first time Bill saw him clearly. Chrysalis. Not a man, a chrysalis. Brown and wrinkled, a thin shape of a man covered entirely in leathery skin. Even his head. But the skin had shrunk to the skull and was smooth, so smooth that the head was faceless without eye sockets or mouth. Yet the head saw him and it snarled.

Bill's nerve broke. He threw his stick, but weakly as though he wanted the man to see he meant no harm and it clattered harmlessly among the branches.

But the sound that came from the faceless head was worse than anything that had come before. A poisonous hiss. And the thin limbs began to move. Bill turned and ran. There was no bravery in him.

The others had followed and were not far behind. His terror swept them up and they ran through the trees, bunched together, pursued by spidery legs.

They blundered on to the heath, threshing through the ferns. They fell and rose again, stumbled and staggered on like swimmers breasting a surf, but separated and hopeless, waiting to be overtaken.

Then a new sound. A hissing in the air. It passed overhead and faded. Behind them the barking of the leather men ceased.

Bill was slightly behind the others. He dared himself to look back. There was nothing in sight. He forced himself to stop. The others floundered on. He stayed where he was, but his head, wide-eyed, jerked from shadow to shadow and each time he was on the verge of running. He knew how it felt to be hunted.

Gradually he calmed the wild movements of his limbs. He tried to stop the others and called out but his voice was no more than a croak. He licked his lips and called again. He thought he heard them stop but suddenly a shape moved in the fog and silenced him. He backed away before it. It was smaller than the leather men. He let it gain on him.

A black fur collar was pulled up so high around her head that only the top half of Elizabeth Goodenough's face could be seen. Bill retreated before her as though the habit of flight would not let him do anything else. She stood still and held out a hand as though she was approaching a frightened animal. Some of Bill's pride returned and he took two trembling steps towards her. The small jewelled hand was still held out to him as though to give help. He put his own hands in his pockets.

Over the parapet of black fur and under the black fringe of her hair, Elizabeth Goodenough's eyes widened, waiting for him to speak. He said nothing.

When she spoke she brought her chin up and narrowed her eyes. It was a nervous habit, as though she was shy.

'I have dispersed them,' she said.

72

'I know you have.' He surprised himself. His voice was low, growling, as though he was angry with her.

The jewelled hands brought a thin, black cigarette case from her pocket, and she put a cigarette between her red lips. She was carrying a little black bag, the strings of which were looped around her wrist, but it was from her pocket that she took an enamelled box containing matches and handed it to him. He struck one for her but had to hold his wrist with his free hand to keep the flame steady.

The others approached cautiously.

'Thank you,' she said, and her eyes became such narrow slits that he could not tell what expression was in them.

7. Inside the House

'Jonquil my dear!'

The cigarette between Elizabeth Goodenough's lips brushed her fur collar as she clasped Jonk's hands in hers. Warm hands, hard rings. Jonk's fear vanished.

Arf came up. Elizabeth looked from him to Bill. Arf was neat, his coat collar turned down, as though the last few minutes had forced him into a rigid shape that was his last hiding place. Bill was hunched, dishevelled, moving his head as though doors had opened in the fog and he did not know which one to go through.

Elizabeth spoke to Jonk. 'I've met your boy friend, but who's the other one?'

No mention of what had just happened. Jonk gave Bill's name first.

'I know,' said Elizabeth.

'I never told you before,' said Jonk.

Elizabeth did not answer. Jonk told her who Arf was and she asked him directly. 'What did you see just now?'

'Two men,' said Arf.

She raised her eyebrows, encouraging him to go on, but Arf was saying no more.

'And you, Bill?'

'He was closer than anybody,' said Jonk.

74

Bill licked his lips. 'Not men,' he said.

'Not men?'

'Well. . . .' He was aware of Arf's spectacles turned on him. 'They were very tall and thin.' He wanted to say their heads had no eyes but this seemed unbelievable. 'They were hooded,' he said, 'and their skin or their clothes – I don't know what it was – was wrinkled stuff like leather.'

'You were close enough to see that?'

He nodded.

Elizabeth was swinging her little black bag by its long strings. He noticed that, in the middle of the heath, she was wearing high-heeled shoes and they were clean.

Arf said, 'I want to know what's going on.'

He was angry at having been frightened, and he was also curious. Bill envied his anger, and let misery submerge him at the thought of how his own bravery had petered out close to the leather men. But Elizabeth looked at him when she said, 'You did well. I've got something to tell you. Come.'

They followed her back through the trees. Bill looked at Jonk for the first time since they were split up by the leather men. She was quiet but did not any longer seem afraid. She had twice been in danger in this place and twice been rescued. It was familiar to her.

Only Jonk had been in the shrub garden, and that had been after dark. As they came through the gate in the wall she felt its power stronger than before. There was soft sand underfoot. A huge wheel of sand, bare except for the dark lines of shrubs. The house was a hump in the centre, the long slope of its roof running down until it almost touched the ground.

Bill also knew they had reached a place of safety, but Arf was uncomfortable. There was something here he could not understand. The fog clung to the trees but within the wall it had thinned so that the circular garden was surrounded by a wall of brick and a tall hedge of trees and grey vapour. The great flat ring cut into the middle of the forest was too wide and the shrubs were too low. He felt that his weight on the edge would make the whole arena tilt. He wanted to get out, but the others were walking through the maze of paths. Why did they have their heads bowed? Why were they so silent? They were like figures in a dream moving with a purpose he could not fathom.

The white sand sucked at his feet. He had to clench his fists and his teeth before he dared step forward, and as he moved he swayed.

The three stood in the porch waiting. Arf felt cold sweat on his forehead as he came up to them. They neither spoke nor smiled. They were like people in a boat looking at him in the water and not realizing he could not swim. But he got to them unaided, and they turned and went into the house.

Inside, everything was subdued. It was warm and a clock ticked gently in a dim corner of the hall. Several doors opened from the hall, and Elizabeth led them into the room Jonk knew. The leaded windows let in little of the grey light from outside, but a big fire was flickering on the wide fireplace. A copper kettle was steaming beside the flames and a teapot was warming on the hearth.

Elizabeth took off her coat and told them to do the same. Then she took teacups from a cabinet.

'Magic consists of putting things in the right order,' she said.

Arf sat down while the others remained standing. She smiled at him.

'All right,' she said. '*Science* consists of putting things in the right order.'

Arf had sat down because he was still trembling from the walk across the strange garden. She seemed to think he was showing he was independent. He did not waste his chance.

'I want to know what's happening,' he said.

'This one takes a lot of convincing,' she said and smiled at Jonk and Bill.

'Mrs Goodenough . . .' Arf began.

'Call me Elizabeth,' she said, 'and pour the tea, there's a good boy.'

'It's not made,' he said.

'Yes it is, enough for four.' She glanced sideways at the other two. 'I like him,' she said, 'he's not going to believe a word I say.'

They drank their tea and for a time nobody spoke. Then Bill said, 'Just before the leather men disappeared there was a rushing sound in the air.'

Elizabeth threw her cigarette into the fire. She did not answer him directly.

'A very long time ago,' she said, 'in this part of the

country from the backlands to the coast there was a struggle between great powers that was never properly ended. But now it has been resumed, and you have become involved in the final act. Which,' she said, tilting her chin and looking at Arf, 'is nonsense.'

It was a sort of compliment. Arf nodded and gave a faint smile.

Elizabeth said, 'I was involved in it from the first because I have lived here a very long time.'

'You must have,' said Arf.

'Drink your tea,' said Elizabeth.

Jonk and Bill were glad to have something to do because Arf was turning out to be an embarrassment. They lifted their cups and drank, but Arf did not do so. He thought it might be drugged.

His attitude did not disturb Elizabeth. She said, 'Now I'll continue. There was a time when this part of the country was fortunate. Nothing disturbed it; nothing for generations. But then a creature came from over the sea, a warlord. He had been displaced from his own country and he came with a gang of knights who offered nothing but the sword. They fought their way steadily inland and they dragged their boat with them as a sign that they would stay.'

Her face was bitter.

'That boat,' she said, 'was pitch black and as it lurched inland, hauled on its rollers first by the knights themselves and later by their slaves, it rested each night in some conquered place so that the black dragon's head at its prow snarled over the roof-tops.'

Elizabeth paused, and when she began speaking again

she was agitated as though blaming herself for something.

'And there was worse than the boat,' she said, 'and I should have known – I should have known.'

It was then that Arf, at his cruellest, interrupted.

'Not you,' he said. 'You are only telling the story.'

Jonk held her breath, and Bill clenched his fists, but Elizabeth did nothing. She did not even look at Arf as she continued her story.

'Those of us,' she said, 'who are set to watch over an area have certain powers, but we are reluctant to use them because they are so potent they are dangerous, and if put to too great use they diminish. They are a last resort. So the people fought unaided in the path of the black boat because I did not know that their enemies were more than ordinary marauders. But there came a day when the warlord and his knights fought a battle against ten times their number and were victors, and in the lonely place where so many died they left the boat as a monument to their victory and marched, unencumbered, to the place from which they would rule the defeated people.

'It was then that the secret of the warlord's power was revealed and it was too late. There was great magic in the belt he wore, and in all the time it had gone undetected it had fixed itself in this country with many deep and devious links.'

There was another pause but this time Arf did not break in.

'The warlord had a palace,' Elizabeth continued, 'which has long since crumbled and been built over.'

'In the city?' It was Bill who asked the question. No matter how strange the little woman's story was, parts of it in some way seemed to fit what was already in his mind.

'In the city,' said Elizabeth. 'From it, he and his knights – knights! they were more brutal than wolves and they fawned on him like dogs – but he and they ruled the land with a grip of iron. But iron rusts, and in the year – do you want the exact year?'

'Yes,' Bill said, answering more to prevent Arf speaking than for anything else.

'It was three years after the coast lands were flooded by black water – three years after the Black Flood.'

Jonk glanced at Bill. If he had wanted to ask more questions she would have interrupted, but he was silent.

Elizabeth had her hands under her chin and they moved jerkily in a way that Jonk remembered. The jewels caught the firelight. They blazed. Arf knew what she was doing; it was a hypnotist's trick to hold his attention as she tried to tell them something even more fantastic. He looked instead into the fire.

A slab of coal lay in the centre, dividing the flames. Its black surface, like a frozen lake, reflected each leaping yellow flag of fire. It interested him to imagine himself walking over the black ice with the yellow forest tossing its branches high overhead. He let his mind wander into it.

Elizabeth put her top lip over the lower. It gave her a look of satisfaction.

'The Black Flood,' she said, her eyes on Arf.

Smoke poured over the coal. Now he wanted to look away, but the torrent of smoke curled in ropes, thick to his sight, and something new that he must see seemed always on the point of boiling to the surface. And all the time he had to listen to her words.

Bill saw all that happened. He watched Arf struggle not to be involved and saw him defeated. Jonk's lips were slightly parted. He had expected her eyes to be wide and vacant, but they were not. She was leaning forward and her eyes, like Elizabeth's, were glinting with firelight as they both looked at Arf.

Bill knew, before they moved, that their heads would turn towards him. Their faces were without expression. Jonk was Elizabeth's creature now, and together they were to snare him. He wanted to struggle, but curiosity overcame him. He sat still and gazed at Jonk. Her eyelashes were long and very black; black as soot; soft and black.

A wind moaned in the chimney and the fire flared. Flared, but the room grew cold. And it appeared to darken as though, as Elizabeth talked, the ice of ancient winters sucked up the fire and diminished it to a cold and tiny gleam.

They were with her in the backlands of long ago when she was preparing to unfasten by magic the warlord's grip on the land. In winter, when ice blackened the ground and the trees and the grass stood stiff, they tested their full strength. His figure loomed broad and terrible, dark except for the bronze belt that glittered against his black armour.

It was a war of terrible silence. Their struggle ranged

wide and the creaking air over the frozen fields balanced first on her side and then on his until, as a winter dawn broke bleakly, the warlord's power over the people cracked and he fled the palace. But she had been unable to tear the belt from him, and it disappeared with him.

There was peace, and the palace was levelled and built over. Far away in the West, with few of his knights left but with the strength of the belt remaining with him, the warlord found a place to lurk. On a green hill on which the figure of a man had been cut to make a ceremonial place, he squatted. His knights, grown scrawny, their features withering away, brought a chill evil to the hill and people grew afraid and did not come near. The forest thickened and at length closed around it with brambles nobody could penetrate.

Many a year of silence. Then a storm thundered in the sky and, as the rains washed villages away in yellow floods, the Green Man heaved himself from his hill and walked. And the warlord rode on him to recover his kingdom.

As Elizabeth spoke they saw it all, but now her voice became words in the room.

'On the borders we met again, in the place you know of, the place of the great battle around the boat. But now I had knowledge to combat the belt. I laid my hand on it and it shattered and my enemy was defeated and fled. The belt lay broken, but that was not the end of it, for now it contained within its parts both his power and mine, and they were still at war. I could not destroy it utterly for my strength was drained. I lay for a long time among the broken pieces and when at length I roused myself they had gone; the belt had escaped us both.

'A broken thing, at war within itself, it hid. But some day it had to be joined. The day is near and the danger grows. For the buckle shall decide which of us shall rule – and the buckle is now seeking out the remainder of the belt.

'Listen to me now and do not forget my words. If, when the belt is worn, the buckle is upright, my power shall prevail. But if the wearer should but stumble and fall so that the buckle's head shall point towards the ground, then nothing can prevent it working great evil. Remember this – in the completed belt the buckle's head must point towards the sky.'

Her words ended. Arf sat gazing into the fire, cut off from the others. But slowly the ropes of smoke released him and he stood up. He and Bill were alone.

Arf frowned. 'I didn't see them go,' he said.

'They told us to wait,' said Bill.

'That woman's full of tricks,' said Arf.

Bill did not reply. He did not throw off dreams as quickly as Arf, and this one was not to be thrust away. It was best to live in it.

'Tricks!' said Arf. 'Cranks in the forest. Dressed up. Scaring each other half to death.'

'And me,' said Bill.

'That's what I mean,' said Arf. 'They are dangerous to some people.'

Elizabeth came back with Jonk.

'Where have you been?' said Arf.

They began putting on their coats before Elizabeth answered.

'Not yet convinced?' she said.

'What of?' said Arf.

'Magic,' said Elizabeth.

'Ha!'

Elizabeth and Jonk looked at each other and laughed. Elizabeth put her hand on Jonk's arm and said, 'When you think the time is ripe, convince him!'

Outside, the wind had cleared the fog, and winter sunshine glared on the white sand. On the doorstep, terror returned to Arf. The shrubs were dark, as black as though they had been burnt. The patterns they made were wicked, yet the others seemed to notice nothing. He held back, and it was not until Elizabeth touched him that he dared move. She stayed close to him all the way to the gate and when it opened he went through and would not look back.

Sunlight pierced the forest and the branches stirred slightly. It was no longer a dead place, and they knew without being told that there was nothing, for the time being, to fear.

Elizabeth left them at the gate. When they reached the first bend in the path and looked back the gate had shut.

And it was then that Arf saw clearer than ever how mad everything was. The leather men, or whatever they were, had been entirely unexplained. A ridiculous story about a long-dead warlord had been forced into their heads, and now they had been pushed out into the forest to wander aimlessly. He stopped.

'What on earth are we supposed to do now?' he said.

Bill, still moving within the dream, roused himself. He also appeared puzzled.

'I've got to get the buckle I found on the Green Man,' said Jonk.

'Why?' asked Arf.

'To bring it back to Elizabeth, of course.'

'Why?'

'Because the warlord has returned,' she said.

8. Elizabeth's Gift

As they got nearer the road and could see the traffic Arf shook off almost all of the strange atmosphere of the house and his questions became more searching. But Jonk was silent and Bill, although more on her side than Arf's, refused to commit himself when Arf tried to make him say one way or the other whether he believed what they had been told or not.

'It's a load of rubbish,' said Arf. 'A lot of cranks pretending that some ancient villain has returned just because a "magic belt" has turned up again.'

'But it makes a sort of sense,' said Bill.

'Sense!' Arf's voice rose to a high note of disbelief.

'Well anyway,' Bill said, 'we've promised to take the buckle to Elizabeth.' He very much wanted Arf to stop talking.

'You promised, not I,' said Arf. 'I think we ought to report the whole thing to the police.'

Jonk's thoughts had been far away, but she spun towards him. 'Shut up!' she said. 'There's one thing neither of you know!'

'And what is that?' said Arf.

'I'll tell you when I have to.'

'Oh lordy-lordy,' said Arf.

She frowned, looking from one to the other.

86

'Why can't you tell us now?' asked Bill.

'Because I was told to wait until we were clear of the backlands.'

Bill accepted this but Arf was scornful.

'You two would fall for anything,' he said.

'Just wait,' said Jonk.

It was a girl's trick. She shut her mouth on her secret and Bill knew that the more they tried to find out, the more firmly her lips would stay sealed.

The sky was blue and clear. Behind them the dark line of the forest was like a mysterious shore seen from the sea, and away to their right the sun glinted on the red of the bus as it sailed towards them.

They asked for tickets for the city. Jonk hesitated, as though she intended to ask for something else, but then she paid her fare and sat looking out of the window, not wanting to talk.

The backlands petered out. They went through a village and turned off the main road, heading for a hamlet where the bus would stop to pick up more passengers. There were fields on either side of the road, no houses.

It was then that Jonk stopped the bus.

'You've got tickets to the city,' said the conductor.

'Doesn't matter,' said Jonk. 'I know where we can get a lift.' This seemed to amuse her and for the first time since leaving Elizabeth she smiled.

They waited on the verge until the bus was out of sight.

Jonk sighed. 'That's better,' she said. She looked both ways along the road. It was a lane with a bank and hedge on each side. Bill and Arf began to ask questions but all

87

she said was, 'I'll show you in a minute. Come on.'

They followed her back down the lane to a gate in the bank. She leant over it, looking around a field of rough grass.

'This'll do,' she said, and pushed the gate open.

'What's all this about?' said Arf.

Still she gave him no answer. She closed the gate behind them and led them along by the hedge. Half-way along she stopped where the hedge was heightened by a line of trees. It was a lonely place, hidden half-way between the backlands and the city.

'Can you tell us now?' said Bill.

'Stay there,' she said, and she herself walked out into the field.

About ten yards away she turned round and pulled from her raincoat pocket a little black bag with long strings. Bill recognized it.

'That's Elizabeth Goodenough's,' he said to Arf.

'So what,' said Arf.

The strings of the bag formed two loops. Jonk put her arms through them and settled the bag between her shoulders like a little haversack. Her long hair had fallen across her face. She pushed it back. She was pale and very tense.

A car went by in the lane behind them. She waited until it had gone, and then reached behind her head, fumbled for a moment and slowly extended her arms, pulling out two more cords from the bag.

Bill caught his breath.

'What's up?' said Arf.

'Look at that!'

Bill was leaning forward, pointing at Jonk. She, with her arms outstretched, was gazing at him, smiling, her eyes shining. Behind her arms, as though the winter sun had coaxed a heat haze from the ground, the air shimmered.

But Arf could see nothing of it. Then a breeze pushed through the hedge at their backs and Jonk was for a moment unsteady on her feet. She seemed alarmed, and then she laughed.

'It nearly pushed me over,' she said.

The wet grass glittered. Bill was laughing with Jonk. Arf saw the bare field stretching away from him and suddenly, like Elizabeth Goodenough's garden, it seemed full of danger.

Jonk and Bill fell silent. She reached above her head and brought her arms down smoothly in a wide sweep. Her feet lifted above the tips of the grass and settled again.

Bill stamped the ground. 'She's flying!' he yelled.

Arf, pale, had to force his mouth to form the words. 'She jumped,' he said.

Jonk reached higher, standing on tiptoe, and brought her arms down again, but faster. She rose a yard into the air and this time did not sink back. Moving her arms in a sort of wide swimming stroke she rose slightly higher and began to move away from them.

Bill ran towards her, but she went away faster and faster. He looked for wings but it was her arms that held her in the air.

He was still running when she reached the end of the field. There was a clear space between her and the hedge beneath. She checked and turned, arms spread wide against the distant blue of the sky. He stopped and held himself on tiptoe, almost airborne himself, afraid that she would reach wrongly in the air and fall. But she turned into the breeze and lifted on it before she thrust back towards him, higher and faster. His mouth was open as he tilted back his head to watch. She went over him with the rushing sound he had heard on the heath just before the leather men had vanished. She swept in a circle and halted almost directly overhead. She held the air with wide arms, her fingers feeling it like the tips of a rook's wings, and came down in front of him.

She stood where she was, on her toes. She let the cords slip from her hands and brought her arms to her sides. Then she stepped towards him. She put out a hand and he held it. It was as cold as a bird's claw. He shuddered. It was no dream.

Hairs blown by the wind of her flight made a thin net on her forehead.

'You can fly,' was all he said.

She nodded, biting her lip.

'Let go of my hand,' she said.

He released it. From her pockets she pulled two more of the little black bags.

'One for Arf,' she said.

Arf stood by the hedge at a distance from them, forlorn and small. They walked towards him, saying nothing but from time to time glancing at each other, wanting to laugh and shout but too anxious to make a sound that might break the spell.

Arf did not want to take the bag. Jonk put it on the

ground by his feet. Bill had the loops over his shoulders and was reaching for the cords when Jonk stopped him.

'You're too near the hedge,' she said.

As he stepped past her he suddenly felt weak. His legs were heavy and clumsy. Doubts made him stumble. He would never get clear of the ground. He walked a long way out before he turned to face the breeze. He felt the sadness that comes after a pleasant dream. He reached behind his head and pulled the loops. They came easily as he extended his arms and he looked over his shoulder to see if the air shimmered. Nothing. He would not make a fool of himself by flapping his arms, but he took a step forward, keeping them stiff.

Was there a slight lift? No; just imagination.

Once more. If this really was a dream he would will himself into the air. He went forward smoothly, slightly faster. His arms were arms, as useful as sticks. His foot caught a tuft of grass and he stumbled. His other foot came forward to take his weight – but it missed the ground. He lurched, seeking something solid with his feet but they sliced air inches from the ground. Down; he wanted to be down. The breeze pressed his face for just an instant. He was lifted gently backwards and sank to earth.

It's true! Don't look at anybody. Force yourself into the air. Here comes the breeze. Treat it like a wave.

He swam into it. He did a slow step in the air, watching the grass slide just beyond reach of his feet. He felt the air in his fingers and made another stroke. It was as though he had grown giddily tall. His head was horse's height above the ground.

He reached forward and up and made another stroke.
He rose without effort. Jonk was ahead. He flew towards
her.

'Turn!' she shouted.

He dipped an arm and swung. It was clumsy; too
sharp. And now the breeze was behind him. He was falling.

He spoke in his mind again: Reach wide with your
arms. Fly faster.

He thrust fiercely and surged forward as he lost height.
His feet were ready for the thud, but just as they brushed
the top of the grass he overtook the breeze and began to
lift. Another pull sent him sloping up. At a safe height
he turned again. He brought himself up gently into
the face of the breeze and let it slow him. He sank to
earth.

He was half-way across the field, grinning, ready to
shout. But he saw Arf.

Arf had started out. While Jonk was watching Bill he
had put the bag between his shoulders and pulled the
cords. The first Bill saw of him he was on his hands and
knees. Jonk stood behind him doing nothing. Bill was
puzzled. Then she bent over, hugging herself, and he
heard the distant sound of her laughter.

Arf got to his feet. Jonk stood back. A wild flapping of
the arms and Arf rose, knees bent. He began to tilt backwards. And then he started to pedal with his feet as
though he was riding an invisible bicycle. Slowly, very
slowly, on his back and pedalling madly, he sank to
earth. Jonk sank with him until she knelt, her hair over
her face, laughing until she was weak.

Bill, standing upright with his arms outstretched, roared.

Arf got up. They held their laughter. Determination was Arf's strength. He stood stiffly, collecting himself. As though moving by numbers he lifted his arms and brought them slowly down. His legs were stiff as he rose straight upwards like a wooden soldier hoisted on a string. Their laughter burst out. Arf struck down again and rose another yard. Concentrating, he jerked himself another yard, then another and another. He was house-height and rising.

'Arf!' they shouted against their laughter. 'Come down!'

He went on climbing.

'Come down!'

He would do something clumsy and kill himself. Their laughter stopped.

At twice house-height, Arf performed the next stage of his plan. Arms out and a slow beat. He moved forward, legs dangling. Then a glide. They heard his voice in the sky: 'I can fly!'

They climbed up with him and circled, calling to each other. The breeze pushed them over the hedge, away from the grass field and over ploughed land.

The nearest houses were distant. They climbed. They could see the city, a jagged dark outline on the horizon. For a time they ignored it. They stretched their legs behind them and found they could lie in the air without effort and their arms felt no weight.

They cut big circles against the sky. Sometimes, as one or other wheeled by, dipping suddenly towards earth, they had a moment of giddiness and would go rigid, expecting arms to become mere arms, and the other dream, the sickening plunge, to dash them down. But always they hung in the air.

Arf's flight was now less jerky. He flew fast down wind, turned in a smooth arc and hung above the other two who were resting on the face of the breeze. They seemed huge, their limbs stretching over fields, forests and roads. It was interesting to see them like this. All of these sensations were interesting. He would eventually find out how the trick was done.

He turned his eyes towards the backlands. The forest was black. The landscape between it and the city undulated slightly, patterned by hedges. He saw things which could not be seen from the road – tracks across fields, a stream with bridges for cattle to cross, a plantation with a clearing in the middle. It was a hidden land in the ordinary world.

'Dark soon,' he called down to them. The hedges were already throwing shadows like a maze of hidden paths.

They turned their heads towards him and the sun caught their eyes and made them glitter. They did not look like his friends. Without a word they wheeled together and sped off down the breeze. Arf was left momentarily alone.

Poised in the hard, cold sky, he suddenly believed in none of it. If he stood still and thought about it he would find he was still on the ground. He put his arms by his sides. The air rushed past him. He panicked and tried to kneel, clutching for the grass he believed he had never left. The air pressed his arms wider and the rushing stopped. He lifted, caught in a strong current. It was like sliding over a polished table, and he pressed himself on to the smooth air. He held his arms still in the safety of the air and went higher. At length he manoeuvred himself round and looked down.

The two below him were as small as birds. He tilted after them, bending his elbows slightly to increase the speed of his dive. He could almost see the air in a long slope ahead and he slid down it faster and faster until he could feel his glasses pushed back against his face. He engineered a shallow scoop at the end of his dive that sent him up again and he closed his arms so that when he lost speed he could just feel himself beginning to drop before he reached out and held himself.

They came down in a field. Arf was almost singing.

'I could do it all day,' he said. 'Let's go up again.'

They seemed not to hear him. They were thinking beyond flying. To one side of the field the sun was sinking, a fierce furnace mouth that was already being shut by the horizon, but above the trees on the other side the moon hung in the deepening blue.

'We shan't get back before nightfall,' said Bill.

'The city is dangerous then,' said Jonk.

They seemed to Arf to be separated from him, as though they had set out in a strange land that he had been reluctant to enter and had left him behind. He tried to catch up.

'Why can't Elizabeth Goodenough fetch the buckle herself?' he said. 'She can do what we can, can't she?'

'Fly, you mean?' said Jonk.

'Yes.'

'Of course she can. She and us. But she must stay near the Green Man.'

'Why?'

'When the Green Man walks, the warlord will be there. She has to meet him.'

Arf was on the point of arguing, but instead he closed his mouth and nodded.

'Where's the day gone?' said Bill. 'A minute or two ago it was morning.'

'We must have been flying a long time,' said Arf.

Bill swung his head from the sun to the moon. They were in a valley of twilight between them.

'Elizabeth told me,' said Jonk, 'we would not be attacked outside the city, but she said once we were inside the walls we were in the warlord's territory. We have to get the buckle out as quickly as we can.'

They walked for a mile along the road before a bus overtook them and they waved it down. It was like getting into a bright barge sailing through the rivers of the night. They let it take them to the next mystery.

9. *Walled In*

The bus entered the city and the traffic closed around it. When they reached the shops the pavements were crowded, and at every gap in the traffic people swirled across the road.

Because they had been warned of danger they got off the bus where the lights were brightest.

'We could have flown all the way if we'd waited a bit longer,' said Bill.

'In the dark?' said Jonk. 'And anyway somebody would have been bound to see us coming down.'

'I feel I'm being watched now,' he said.

The crowds were hurrying by, nobody paying any attention to them, but now they began to notice things they had not been aware of. There were many places, even in the centre of the city, from which they could be observed. A row of tall pillars along the front of a bank reminded them of the winter forest, there were steps going up to dark doorways, and lightless windows above street level could contain many hidden watchers.

Away from the city centre it was worse. Houses that stood back in the darkness gazed at them as they went by, and streets they had never explored seemed to lead to silent, secret places where few people had ever been.

They went cautiously, often stopping and occasionally

running along a stretch that seemed particularly menacing, but they reached Jonk's gate without anything happening.

With the immediate danger past and the memory of flying still strong in them they were exhilarated.

'The sooner we can get going again, the better,' said Bill. 'Will you be able to get out again all right, Jonk, as soon as you've got the buckle?'

'I'll manage it somehow.'

'We'll wait for you.'

'Blow that,' said Arf. 'I need something to eat.'

He was right – and they had also to explain why they had not been home all day. They stood for a moment thinking out their excuses, but suddenly Arf said, 'Why don't we just tell them the truth?'

'You're daft,' said Bill. 'Who'd believe us?'

'But we could show them we can fly.'

'No!' said Jonk.

Bill glanced quickly at her. She knew that flying was for themselves alone, and he knew she was right but he could also see the strength of Arf's case. He was caught between them yet again. He sighed.

'We haven't time,' he said to Arf. 'Just think how long it would take them to get used to it.'

'Well I don't know,' said Arf.

He was not quite convinced and wanted to argue, but Bill said quickly, 'And remember, Elizabeth's power isn't limitless. Whatever is in these bags can be used up. We know we can fly, that's all that matters.'

'Of course it is,' said Jonk, impatient to get on with what they had to do.

Arf shrugged. Their arguments did not bear examination, but neither did flying. He was already doubting that he had done it.

They parted without saying anything more.

When Jonk got indoors her mother was angry.

'And where have you been all day, my girl?'

'Shopping.'

'All day? You can't tell me you've been shopping all day. And what about your dinner?'

'I had some up the city, and it took me a long time to choose something for you.'

Her mother's present was already hidden upstairs, but the lie seemed justified and it worked. Her mother smiled and shook her head.

'Well it was naughty,' she said. 'I was worried about you.'

'No need to be, Mum. I'm protected.'

'What on earth do you mean by that?'

'Secrets.'

'You kids!'

Off-handedly, Jonk said, 'I've got to go out after tea.'

'Oh no you haven't!'

'But I've got to!'

'There's no "got" about it. Besides I saw . . .'

Her mother, bustling about in the kitchen, did not finish the sentence.

'What did you see, Mum?'

'Nothing. I just don't want you to go out after dark, that's all.'

'But why not?'

99

There was no reply.

'Why not?' Jonk was frowning.

'It's no use you getting cross. It's just that after what happened yesterday I don't like the thought of you going out alone, not when there are big black dogs about. There now.'

'What dogs?'

Jonk had gone pale. Her mother was looking at her sharply.

'I thought that would change your tune. There's been a horrible dog roaming about all afternoon. I came out of the door and there it was at the garden gate, staring at me. Horrible wicked eyes.'

'What happened? Was there anybody with it?'

'Not that I could see. I saw it several times up and down the road. Great big thing roaming wild like that! I'm going to tell your father about it when he gets home.'

Jonk was silent. It was the first sign of danger since they had left Elizabeth. Suddenly she thought of the buckle. She went quickly out of the room. Half-way up the stairs she wished she had put the light on. It was dark and cold, like being in another house. Somebody was leaning over the banisters. She almost cried out, but held her voice back just in time. The leaning figure was a coat. She hurried past it, holding her breath until she thrust her hand under the mattress of her bed and felt the buckle. It was icy.

She had to get out of the house, but it was far from easy. To make it more difficult, Jane would not leave her alone.

'Go away,' said Jonk. 'This kid is always getting under your feet.'

'Don't talk to your sister like that,' said her mother.

'You do.'

It was a mistake she would never have made if she had been less harassed. Her mother's anger returned, and when Jonk had bolted some tea and started to get ready to go out she forbade her.

'But they'll be waiting,' Jonk pleaded.

'They can wait all night. It's no use putting on a face like that. And you can just sit down and have a proper tea before anything is decided at all.'

'Where are you going?' asked Jane.

'It's no use asking her, my pet,' said her mother. 'It's all secrets with her at the moment.'

There was a knock at the door.

'That's them,' said Jonk.

'Just you wait there,' said her mother.

It was now or never. Jonk put her coat on and filled her pockets with food. She was behind her mother as she opened the door to Bill. Before anybody had a chance to speak, Jonk held her mother's hand and said in the most appealing way she could, 'Let me go, please. It *is* Christmas.'

'Minx!'

There was a half-smile on Mrs Winters' face.

'Thank you, Mum.' Jonk was outside and hurrying up the path before anything happened to stop her.

'I had a job to get out as well,' said Bill.

It was a cold, bright night. At the gate, Jonk looked quickly up and down the street. It was empty.

'Thank goodness for that,' she said.

'What do you mean?' Bill asked.

'My mother's seen the dog.'

'Your mother?'

Jonk nodded. Neither needed to speak about it. If others were now able to see the dog it meant the threat was growing. When Arf joined them, Jonk told him what had happened. It made them move warily, but once again nothing threatened them as they crossed the city, and they got to the bus station with time to spare.

The bus was crowded with people leaving the city after a day's shopping. The luggage racks were crammed and paper was rustling everywhere. They felt out of place. On the top deck there were fewer people, and the front seats were empty. They sat there eating what food they had been able to smuggle from home and waited for the bus to leave. They said little.

At last the bus lurched out into the traffic. It was a slow journey through the centre of the city, but they did not mind. In the afternoon it had been easy to say they would return with the buckle; now the thought of the backlands after dark was already testing their nerve.

They looked out of the windows hardly expecting danger now that they had twice walked through the city without trouble. Elizabeth's warning had perhaps made them too cautious. But Jonk suddenly stiffened.

'What?' Bill kept his voice low, forcing himself to sound calm.

She nodded, pointing with her eyes.

Keeping just ahead of the bus, a black dog was snaking

through the crowds on the pavement. Like a dolphin alongside a ship it kept pace with them.

'May not be the one,' said Bill.

Jonk shook her head. She knew better.

The bus, reaching a clearer road, began to gather speed. The dog kept with them. Bill reached across the gangway and tugged Arf's sleeve. Arf leant across.

'See it?' Bill asked.

'Yes. What are we going to do?'

Bill folded his arms across his stomach and leaned forward, bunched up, hugging himself. His mind was fitting something together.

'What we are going to do,' he said slowly. Then he paused. The idea had not yet revealed itself. 'What we are going to do,' he repeated, and paused again. His eyes were on the dog running ahead as he forced his thoughts together.

'Got it!' He launched himself forward, pressing his face to the window with his hands cupped around his eyes. He stayed like that for no more than two seconds then, moving just as suddenly, he stood up.

'We are getting off. Come on, quick!'

They followed him down the gangway but he was on the platform paying the conductor as they reached the top of the stairs.

'Can you see the dog?' he shouted. There was no attempt at secrecy.

'No,' Arf called down. 'Too much traffic.'

The bus stopped. They jumped off and were running in the opposite direction before it started.

'What are we doing?' said Jonk, running alongside Bill.

He did not answer, but in the shadow of a tree that leaned out from a garden he stopped them.

'Look.' He pointed back up the road.

They caught a glimpse of the dog. It was still with the bus, but lagging.

'It knows we aren't on it,' said Jonk. 'It'll come back after us.'

'I'm not bothered about that,' said Bill. 'Look ahead of the bus. See?'

At the side of the road, jutting out on to the pavement, was a ruined flint tower. Little more than a stump of it remained.

'City wall,' said Bill. 'They'd never let us past that.'

'We'd have got by on the bus,' said Arf.

The ruin was almost all that remained of the wall after many centuries. It was now no sort of barrier. The bus drew level with it. There was little traffic on the roads and they could hear its engine clearly. Suddenly it coughed then revved up and cut out. The bus stopped. They heard the starting motor whine feverishly but the engine was dead.

The dog stood by it, confused, turning its head this way and that.

'It'll see us!' said Jonk. 'Let's go now.'

She was right. The dog's head levelled at them and it began to leave the bus. The shadow of the tree was no protection. They began to back away.

And then, in the blackness by the ruined tower, there was a movement. They heard a whistle. Jonk caught her

breath. Somebody had whistled in the forest after
Elizabeth had saved her from the dog. The dog stopped
and looked back. When the whistle came again it turned
and moved away.

At the same instant the starting motor of the bus
whined again and immediately the engine started. After a
moment the bus gingerly moved off. It was as though it
moved merely to distract them. When they looked for
the dog again it had gone.

'That was close!' Bill, discovering he had been in a half-
crouch ready to run, straightened.

Jonk made a weak little flapping motion with one
hand. 'Oh,' she said. 'How did you know it was going to
happen?'

'Guessed.' But it was more than a guess. Bill had feelers
out in the night.

'So,' said Arf, 'we're fenced in, is that it?'

'Looks like it,' said Bill. 'And you know what the next
thing will be.'

'Yes,' said Jonk.

'What?' said Arf.

'The buckle. All they're doing at the moment is seeing
we don't get out with it. But when it suits them – when
we're alone somewhere – they'll come for it.'

'Let's get where there's more light,' said Jonk.

They began to walk towards the centre of the city.

'We'll have to fly, then,' said Arf.

'Yes,' said Bill, 'but we can't go straight away. It might
be a long job and we'd better think it out first.' He looked
up at the sky and watched his breath cloud the stars.
'And it's cold up there. We need better clothes.'

'But it has to be tonight,' said Jonk. 'I daren't sleep with that buckle in my room.'

Arf made as though to say something then changed his mind. But Bill noticed and asked him what it was.

'Well I've got a compass we could use and my father's got a good map, but the trouble is once we get home we'll never get out again.'

'Yes we can,' said Bill. 'After they've all gone to bed.'

Jonk shivered. 'I don't fancy that,' she said.

'There's no other way.'

She hung her head and her hair swung forward to hide her face. They walked on in silence, but after a time she lifted her head and brushed her hair back.

'All right,' she said. 'Let's go to Arf's and see the map.'

10. Night Flying

The night creaked. It was bitterly cold. Jonk lay in bed staring at the ceiling. If she kept her light on she would be certain to stay awake. Her bed was warm and the sheets were up to her mouth where she liked them. It was difficult to keep her eyes open. She pushed the sheet under her chin. With it like that she dared close her eyes. Her breath came softly and the sheet crept back to her mouth.

Suddenly she jerked her eyes open. There was somebody in her room.

'It's only me,' said her mother. 'Did I give you a fright?'

'You did,' said Jonk.

'Did you know you went to sleep with your light on?'

Asleep? Jonk glanced at the watch on her wrist. It was only half past eleven. She lay back with a sigh. There was time for the house to settle before she need move.

'I don't know what's got into you just lately,' said her mother. She looked worried.

'I'm all right, Mum,' said Jonk. 'Tired, that's all.' She forced a yawn although now she was wide awake.

Her mother put out the light and left. In the darkness Jonk listened until both her mother and father were in bed, and then she got out and dressed, shivering. She sat by the window with her eiderdown around her, ready for a long wait.

Bill had the most difficult task of them all. He shared a room with his brothers. When they were asleep he sat up in bed, put on his shirt and pullover and buttoned his pyjama jacket on top. Then he pulled the bedclothes up to his chin and sat looking out of the window at the roof of Arf's house opposite. He knew he might sleep, but when his parents came in before going to bed he was bound to wake up.

The cold crept around the back of his neck. As he dozed off the coldness reached down his back. He was too uncomfortable to sleep properly and he heard his parents long before the door opened. He slid down and pretended to be asleep until they had gone. Then he sat up and re-arranged himself, but now every part of the bed was cold.

It was after midnight before he heard his father snoring. It was a relief to get out of bed, but he had to move carefully. He dressed, humped the bedclothes to make it appear he was still in bed and, inch by inch, he opened the door and crept along the landing. He spent a long time in the black well of the stairs, feeling his way down backwards, on all fours, and he crouched over the last embers of the living-room fire until it was time to go.

Arf, with an alarm clock under his pillow, slept until a quarter to one.

By that time Jonk was working at the bolt of her front door. It was stiff. She had been growing her fingernails long and one of them broke, painfully. She jumped as Bill, around for their scent before the trees hid it. As they crossed the park boundary, gaining height over the roof-tops, they heard its wolf howl searching the shadows below.

11. Elizabeth's House

They climbed until the roofs of the city lay beneath them like a crumpled carpet patterned by rows of lights. They swam over it, peering down, but they could see nothing moving in the black square of the park.

They flew towards the outskirts, moving gingerly through the icy air in case some barrier extended upwards from the city wall to keep them in, but their toes trailed past the fringes of the lights and they were outside.

They breathed easier and went forward at speed, searching the ground for the road that led to the backlands. But the earth below was dark, a jumble of shadows with here and there a silver glint of the moon on water.

Arf could not use his compass, and they slowed – winnowing with their hands to keep height as they searched for a landmark.

'We'll get lost,' said Bill. 'Let's go down and look at the map.'

They sank towards a field, going down into it suspiciously, feeling, as they got below tree height, that they were being swallowed. Their feet pressed into the frozen grass. The night was absolutely still.

'Cold up there,' said Bill.

Under the moon the frost was a powdery grey, but in

spite of it the earth seemed to give them warmth. They rubbed their hands and arms and then crouched close to shield the light of the torch as they examined the map. They could not be sure where they were but they tried to memorize some of the roads and they took a compass bearing. Then they climbed towards the sky. The landscape was vague and they were wandering uncertainly in the general direction of the backlands when a lorry came from the city and drew a line for them with its headlights along the road they wanted. It soon turned off, but they could see enough to travel fast.

The road was often hidden, sometimes seeming to be squeezed out of existence by the fields, and often impossible to distinguish from hedgerows, but they were always able to pick up its dark band ahead or follow its hidden track by the houses which dotted it like knots in a piece of string.

They flew in line abreast, only a few feet separating their finger-tips. The cold air bit their throats but even though they did not have to make huge strokes with their arms to move at speed it was enough to keep them warm.

At length, however, Jonk called out, 'My arms ache. I'll have to glide.'

'Let's climb first,' said Bill.

'Then we'll go in single file,' said Arf, his voice coming from the face of the moon. He had an idea that birds flew one behind another because this formation made better use of the air currents.

They were panting and their flying was becoming clumsy when they levelled out and lay as though on the top of an invisible hill. Bill tilted and slid away first, followed by Jonk and Arf. There was no strain at all on their outstretched arms and they relaxed their muscles, even resting their necks by letting their heads droop.

Rocking gently above Bill, Jonk dreamed her time away. He seemed motionless below her, like somebody sprawled in sleep. His head was on the horizon and his shape was as dark as the earth beneath, but huge; his hand covered a whole field. When he moved to begin climbing again it was as though he dug himself from the earth in which he was embedded. She remembered the purpose of their flight and went up with him.

Rising and falling, they covered a good mile at each swoop and soon the flat heaths of the backlands lay on both sides of the road. Ahead of them the dark masses of the forest blotted out the ground. They climbed steeply and circled, trying to pick out the track that led from the main road. Several uncertain lines veined the heath.

'Look for the house,' Jonk called.

They spread out and flapped slowly over the matted trees which were pocketed here and there with clearings. The moon, high now, filled every clear space with its light, but every gap in the forest was empty.

Then a corner of heathland seemed familiar to Jonk. Tilting her arms, she curved through the air, gazing down to her left where her finger-tips were drawing a circle round the place she recognized. Bill and Arf came closer.

'This it?' said Bill.

'I think it's where I saw the dog.'

She looked for the grove of trees that surrounded the hand of the Green Man, but there was nothing.

'Sorry,' she said. 'Wrong place.'

But suddenly she checked, arching her arms. She was steady, but losing height, sinking straight down. She studied what she had spotted. The grove was there but it was no longer upright. Its trees lay side by side like grass pressed down in a picnic place. A broad track of torn earth led from it.

The others swooped beside her as she was still picking out the details. She tried to point but rocked wildly and lost height too quickly. She climbed, drawing them with her. When she stopped, they all saw what lay beneath.

The folds of the heath made up a shape. The Green Man was so huge that it was only from this height they could see him whole. The steep sides of his body rose to the flat uplands of his chest and belly, and his legs and arms were like the foothills of a mountain range. One arm lay close to him, making a black chasm between it and his side, and the other was crooked round a wide area of the heath. His legs were thrust into the forest. His head cast a deep shadow but had no eyes, nose or mouth.

They fluttered like larks above him.

'They've cut down your trees to fit his hand in,' said Arf.

'No,' said Jonk, 'he pulled them down himself.'

'Ha!' Arf's reaction was automatic, and then he saw the gashed earth from which the arm had torn itself and he said nothing more.

Jonk knew where to go. A short flight over the black forest brought them to Elizabeth's house and they slid down towards it.

Above the tops of the trees they held back to look

down into the walled garden. The patterns in the sand were very clear and the house in the centre seemed ready to welcome them. They waited for Jonk to lead them down, but still she held back.

Bill edged forward.

'Let's get down there,' he said.

But Jonk flew to and fro, keeping outside the wall. Something was wrong. The house was too dark. It looked uninhabited. And there was something else. The patterns were not the same. The little hedges had surely been neater when she last saw them. She said what was on her mind.

'It's the moonlight,' said Bill. 'It makes everything different.'

He again moved forward and she clutched at him. They both lost their balance and started to fall. They almost hit the trees before they steadied themselves and climbed back to Arf. But he paid them no attention. His eyes did not move from the house.

'I thought I saw something move,' he said. 'Just to the left.'

They forgot their fall. For two minutes they watched, but nothing happened. The house seemed sinister now, and Bill saw that Jonk was not mistaken about the patterns. There were gaps in the shrub rows. He licked his lips and made up his mind.

'Stay here and watch,' he said, and launched himself forward.

'Don't!' Jonk's voice came from the sky behind him as he slanted across the garden.

In two strokes he was over it and swinging his legs forward like a hawk coming in to land on the roof ridge. As his feet touched he spilled the air from his arms and reached for the chimney stack. He was unsteady for a moment, tilting backwards and forwards, but then his hands got a firm grip and he eased himself closer to the brickwork. The loops were a hindrance and he let them go.

It was very quiet. The forest top was above him now, pressing as close to the house as the wall allowed. He could hear a pulsing beat in the air. It came from Jonk and Arf as they held themselves above the trees, and he realized for the first time how much sound they made as they flew. It seemed to come to him from a long way off, like a distant machine that would throb all through the night.

The ridge was not a good position. More of the garden was hidden from him than when he was outside the wall. He turned his head, working out his next move.

The roof was blotched with lichen. The bricks of the chimney were clammy under his gloves. He shivered. One good thing anyway, he thought, there was no smoke coming up in his face. No smoke. There were four chimney pots. He felt each of them. They were all cold. The house was empty; it may have been empty all day. The only way to find out was to fly down.

He leant against the brickwork to steady himself as he reached for the loops and his face was over the sooty mouth of one of the pots. He had an idea. He put his face closer to the black hole.

'Elizabeth Goodenough!' he said. 'Elizabeth Good-enough!'

His whisper was swallowed like a pebble going into mud.

Then a faint sound came from below. It may have been a mouse in the hearth or a cinder settling in the cold grate.

'Elizabeth Goodenough!'

His head was very close to the sooty opening. Suddenly, as though it had been waiting to have his head in its jaws, the black mouth snarled. He jerked back, began to lose his balance, and had to cling tight. For a moment he was unable to move his head and it was caught in the full force of the sound. It grated in his ears louder and louder, entering his head like teeth that would crack him open.

He knew what it was. Leather men, the warlord's shrivelled black knights, had been close to him once before and their voices had made him shrink in front of them.

Slowly, the teeth of the sound pulling at him, he lifted his head. His eyes were glazed, unseeing. All his senses were in his ears. But, as though the sound itself had taken on a shape, something dark moved in the corner of his eye. It seemed to dance, and he turned towards it.

Below, in the garden, a leather man had come from the shadow of the house and was moving towards the outer wall, his long arms jutting out and waving as his legs moved his body smoothly, spider-like, over the shrubs.

Jonk saw the creature and at the same time heard the snarl. She could not help making an armbeat that lifted her back, away from the danger, but instantly she forced herself forward. She was just above the tops of the trees.

Across the open space she could see Bill. Why did he not move?

More leather men spilled from the house and ran over the sand. Like the sea rasping and snarling in dangerous coves, their roar filled the garden.

Bill stood where he was. She could see bare arm between his gloves and the edge of his jacket sleeves. She knew the loops were not in his hands.

Bill was afraid. His head moved stiffly in the din, watching the garden fill up. But the seething black sea of leather men was below him. On the rock of the house he was still safe. He clenched his jaw and waited.

Below the eaves behind him a window opened. He did not see the long thin arms reach out and hook themselves to the gutter.

As though battling through a gale, Jonk crept closer. Arf was behind her and above.

The man-shaped thing slid through the window, the moon giving its smooth head and shoulders a dull gleam. The arms reached higher, found a grip on the tiles, and in a series of insect jerks the leather man eased himself on to the roof.

It was then that Arf saw him, but his yell was broken up in the din. Jonk looked up at him, wobbled, and watched his dive. Then she also saw the danger. She lunged after Arf.

Arf closed his arms until he was falling almost like a stone. Bill's head was twisted towards him. The leather man clawed up the tiles.

Arf passed behind Bill. Bill swung his head to follow

him, and saw a thin arm reaching for the ridge. The black gleaming skull was a yard from him.

Jonk was half-way over the garden when she saw Bill bring his hands from the chimney as Arf sped by in the moonlight behind him. She saw the round head rise over the ridge and an arm reach.

Bill, without the loops in his hands, ran straight down the tiles. His hands went behind his head and grabbed. Because of his gloves he could not tell if he held the cords. His feet clattered on the tiles and he leant out as though he would fly, but not certain that he would.

Arms out. Roof edge. Kick.

He was swallow diving into a swaying mass that reached for him. Down. Something touched his face. He thrashed and kicked and rose.

Like a bullet Arf skimmed the ridge. Jonk crossed from the opposite direction. The three weaved in a swift spiral, out and clear.

Behind them, as they fled over the gaping hollows of the forest, a jagged, frustrated shriek tore at itself in the wide, calm night.

12. The Rescue

They flew high until the forest was behind them. In the distance the lights of the city glittered like hoar frost on a pavement. They said nothing, letting the fear ebb away and waiting for their thoughts to make sense again. Then, without any one of them giving the lead, they pointed themselves towards the ground.

The bare fields were as unattractive as a cold sea; they wanted to be near people. They saw a village clustered near a crossroads, but most of its houses were around the open space of the village green. They rocked gently down from the sky until the grass crunched under their feet and they stood as still as three trees. The cottages were silent, lightless. Within doors, under heaped sheets and eider-downs, people were asleep.

'I wish it would end,' said Jonk. 'Why can't it all be over?'

Bill and Arf stood silently. All three felt sick and weak.

'I don't want to fly any more,' said Jonk. 'I want to walk home.' She was almost crying.

They stepped towards the road. There was a signpost and a little bridge over a stream. Arf shone his torch briefly to read the names. Their road led across the bridge.

Bill paused to look over the parapet. The water rippled

gently over the stones until it came to a dark pool under the bridge where it seemed to linger without any movement. He thought of himself falling into the deep water, the black river bed beyond reach of his feet.

'Swim!' he muttered. 'Swim! Swim!'

Then he turned his eyes furtively on the others, embarrassed. Their faces were blank and he was relieved they had not heard. Then Arf said, 'What did you say?'

'Nothing,' he replied quickly. 'Nothing. Just that we've got to do something.'

They walked on, not speaking.

'Thirteen miles,' said Arf. 'It's a long way to walk.'

The road sloped uphill out of the village. The bitter air stung the inside of their noses, but the effort of climbing made them warmer.

Jonk was the first to mention what had happened.

'The leather men have got Elizabeth,' she said. She wanted to be contradicted, to be told that Elizabeth must have abandoned her house and be roaming somewhere free, but Arf gave her no comfort.

'They must have,' he said.

Bill stayed silent. Twice he had dared the leather men and twice his courage had broken. If he had been braver he might have circled the house, smashed a way in and done something to rescue Elizabeth.

'Bill,' said Jonk.

'What.' He spoke irritably, not wanting her questions. But what she said eased his mind.

'I don't think Elizabeth was there,' she said.

They had breasted the hill above the village and were facing the horizon which hid the city.

'Why not?'

'I don't know. I just feel she wasn't.'

Bill suddenly straightened. His mind leapt ahead.

'No,' he said. 'You're right. She wouldn't be there. They'd take her into the city, to the palace, wherever it is. We've still got a chance.'

'All we've got to do is find it,' said Arf, 'and we haven't got a clue.'

But Bill's black mood had passed. He started to run and they came with him. Three abreast, they ran down the centre of the road and, with him, they reached for the loops.

They spread their arms and suddenly the sound of running feet ended. They mounted the air as though steps stretched up into the sky and when they were out of breath they lay and let themselves drift.

'We've found a current,' said Arf, 'and it's going the right way.'

Bill took it for an omen. 'Our luck's changed,' he said. 'We're going to be all right.'

As though they were in the bows of a ship gazing down into the water they watched the lights of the city float towards them like a patch of foam.

'Something funny about it,' said Bill.

'Looks the same to me,' said Arf.

'Yes, but there's a strip of it blacked out. Can you see?'

'Yes,' said Jonk. 'Almost a straight line. Is it the river?'

'No.' Arf was quite certain. 'That's way over to the south. This is the west.'

'I know what it is,' said Bill. 'It's the city wall.'

'Can't be that,' said Arf. 'There is no city wall.'

'They are putting it back.'

Arf examined the dark band that cut through the lights. 'I can see no wall.'

'It's no-man's-land,' said Bill. 'There's leather men patrolling there for us, bet you what you like.'

Jonk was watching a car approach the city. Its headlights slid into the dark patch and it did not alter speed. It lit up a strip of road she recognized.

'It *is* the city wall,' she said. 'The bus stopped just about where that car is.' She caught a glimpse of the crumbling tower.

The car crossed the darkness and was gone. Its lights had shown that the street was empty. Then from below came a sound that sent them leaping upwards. The crackling snarl of leather men, even from a distance, seemed to claw at them.

There was movement in the darkened strip, but nothing they could distinguish. Then the darkness became more intense. The lights on the road leading out of the city flickered and dimmed, but just before they went out they saw something moving in towards the city from the country.

'Looks like people,' said Arf.

'Spread out,' said Bill. 'We're going down.'

The noise of the leather men swayed up towards them. It drowned the sound of their flight and they descended until they were just clear of the rooftops. There was enough light from the sky to show them the advancing group. It was leather men, formed in a ragged ring and shuffling forward, shoulders almost touching. In the centre, walking alone, was a small figure, Elizabeth.

Jonk swayed towards her. Elizabeth's head was bent. Bill put out a hand to hold Jonk back as Elizabeth raised her eyes. As she did so the street lights flickered and threw a dim yellow light. Elizabeth looked up, straight at Jonk. She did not smile but her eyes caught a glitter of the yellow light. Then her head drooped and the lights flickered once more and went out.

They flew higher, hiding themselves in the sky.

Soon Elizabeth would reach the city wall.

'If we dive now we can break the ring,' said Bill. He dipped and began to fall.

'No!' Jonk cried.

He opened his arms and paused below her. She spoke down at his upturned face.

'She doesn't want us to. She wants to get into the city.'

Bill lurched up towards her and Arf. They held themselves close, in a circle that rose and fell as they fingered the air. In the moonlight their faces were pale, their eyes dark.

'You sure?' said Bill. He saw Jonk's hair sway against her cheeks as she nodded.

'If she wants us she'll call.'

He did not ask her how she knew.

Elizabeth, in the midst of her guards, entered the band of darkness. There was a roar worse than that in the garden as more leather men joined them. The road seethed.

Arf saw another late-travelling car coming from the

country and he drew away from Jonk and Bill to watch. The car stopped. He saw its headlights dim as the driver tried to restart his stalled engine, but the car did not move.

Arf sank lower and peered at the windows of the houses. The din of the leather men must bring people out. But not a curtain stirred. The nightmare they were involved in was private. He climbed back to the others and looked in their faces. They had not bothered to see what would happen to the car; they already accepted that they were on their own.

'She's in the thick of them,' said Bill. 'I can't see her.'

'They're moving off along the wall,' said Jonk.

They followed her as she dipped lower. In the blacked-out roads, figures cut across patches of moonlight. Jonk alone was certain where Elizabeth moved.

They drifted overhead. Bill moved close to Jonk.

'There don't seem so many guarding her now,' he said.

'No need. Not inside the wall.'

'What are we going to do about the buckle?'

'She'll let us know.'

Jonk moved away, concentrating on what was happening below.

They were getting closer to the river. They could see its curves glint in the moonlight. The streets were narrower and the houses were old. There were factories and yards and some warehouses.

Jonk kicked suddenly, turning towards the centre of the city. The group below had left the darkness of the wall.

'King Street,' said Arf.

Bill had forgotten the city was a place they knew. They had even explored this part. The whole area between King Street and the river was black and crumbling. There were boarded up shops and derelict houses that were gradually being cleared for new buildings.

The group below kept to the middle of the street, the shadows of the leather men lengthening and shortening as they went by the few street lamps. In this area they had no need of darkness.

Jonk's armbeats became shorter and tenser. She stretched her head forward, watching and waiting.

Elizabeth stopped. Instantly the leather men closed up. From above they saw her bring her arms up and even caught the glitter of her rings as her hands jerked. The circle of leather men bulged out where she pointed but did not break. Her hand stabbed again. The circle buckled, stretched, swayed inwards and locked tight. Within the city her power was no longer enough.

It was then that she raised her face to the sky. It was a small blur overshadowed by the towering leather men.

Jonk tilted forward but Bill was faster. He had a memory to wipe out. With his fists close to his shoulders he used all his weight to streak from the sky. Hawk-like, feet first, nudging the air with his elbows for direction, he dropped through the whistling air.

The instant before his feet struck he flung his hands wide. The bang of the air against his arms covered the crack and crunch of his feet as he split the ring. Flattened under his feet were two black ruins. He lifted, sliding sideways clear. The hiss and bang of Arf and Jonk came together. The ring was shattered.

They leapt as high as the houses, ready to drop again. There was a quick rap of high heels away to one side as Elizabeth fled. Behind her the long shadows of two leather men reached for her. Their rasping cry was being answered from another street.

They thrust at the air, picking up speed, but not quickly enough. Elizabeth was round a corner and out of sight. A second later the leather men disappeared after her.

They flicked over the roof-tops and dropped to her aid. But there was no target. Nothing. They clustered, hovering. And then they saw, in the middle of the road, lying still, the long forms of two leather men.

'Elizabeth!' Jonk cried.

There was no answer.

Jonk went down and started to run along the empty street, her hair flying behind her.

One of the leather men stirred, long arms vibrating like feelers. His grating cry rattled against the houses. At the corner a black wave of leather men spilled into the street. Their roar spun Jonk round. She thrust herself skywards as they surged beneath.

For a long time they flew over the streets, searching ahead of the leather men as they spread out, penetrating every alley and courtyard, but Elizabeth had disappeared in the heart of the warlord's territory.

'Ha!' said Arf.

'He's himself again anyway,' said Jonk. 'Wish I was.'

They took off. A policeman standing beneath heard a rushing sound and thought something was falling. He cringed away. When he looked up he caught a glimpse of a shape sinking into the stars. Big bird, he thought.

Bill led them to the cathedral. It was a short flight and they had not gained enough height for his purpose when they crossed its roof. The spire was above them, a tapering column standing alone above the city, untouched for years on end, known only to the birds. They circled it, rising, as though they were going up an invisible spiral stair.

The tip was not as sharp as it seemed from the ground. A massive stone held the weight of a great gilded weathercock. It sat motionless on its pivot, its crowing head and plumed tail, made from thick metal, were jagged shapes that had cut into the rain on many a stormy night and had flashed wet gold in the morning sun.

Bill had chosen a good place. Jonk flew towards the weathercock and reached for it with arms and legs. Her feet landed on the bar of the north-pointing arrow below the bird and she threw her arms across its back. The loops in her hands were a hindrance and she released them.

Suddenly she was supporting all her own weight. The weathercock, big though it was, was delicately balanced and it lurched and swung.

On a summer's day she had stood in the Cathedral Close and watched the spire moving against the clouds as though it was toppling from the sky. Now she felt sure it was really falling, unbalanced by the shock of her landing. She clung, experiencing the long, curving plunge of the tall tip. Her eyes were almost closed and she was not breathing.

With a jerk that was the thump of her heart the fall ceased. She looked below. The spire's foot was hidden. The fall began again. She clung and fought her giddiness. Slowly, she steadied the world.

Then Bill came close and held himself steady in the air just beyond the point of the weather vane. The drop below him was enormous. She hated him wildly as the fear of heights clutched her again. She wanted to scream at him, and she mouthed words but her breath was too thin to make a sound. She closed her eyes on him, clenched her teeth and waited for the panic to go.

When her breathing steadied she opened her eyes. Bill came closer.

'Keep away!' she shouted.

He backed off.

'Can't I help?' he called.

'No! I'll do it.'

The weathercock was hollow, its plated sides open at the top. She felt inside. There were iron struts, and just where the plates came together at the breast there was a cavity that would just take her hand as far as the wrist. She brought her other hand inside the bird and held to a strut. Then, using her teeth, she took off her glove and reached for the buckle. She gripped it so hard it bit into her fingers as, stiffly, she raised her arm and brought it back to the cavity.

She put the buckle in. Was it safe? She pressed her glove on top of it, and then she pulled off her scarf and jammed that between the rusty plates as well.

It was only then that she raised her head.

'All right?' Bill and Arf had come close.

She nodded. She was clinging to the weathercock with both hands and did not know how she would get them to the loops behind her head. If she moved, the weathercock would pivot and she would plunge from the bar on which she stood.

Bill and Arf watched her. They saw first one hand then the other make a quick little movement towards her shoulder and then jerk back to cling to the metal bird. Her voice, little more than a whisper, reached them.

'I daren't,' she said. 'I daren't.'

'Hang on, Jonk.' Bill came towards her slowly.

He let himself sink below the bars of the weathervane until he was beneath her, and he flattened himself to the spire, clinging like a bat to small carved crockets on the stonework.

She saw the face below her feet. It was pale, indistinct, like something under water.

He said something. She did not know what the words were. She closed her eyes, willing him to go away, willing her dream to come to an end. He reached up and touched her foot. She started and opened her eyes. The cathedral roof far below was black. The spire pierced the air and ended where she stood. It was no dream. Flying was no dream, and neither was the buckle. And the buckle was no longer with her.

Suddenly she had the courage to act. Straightening, she held the weathercock's back with one hand and stepped out along the bar. She let go and balanced for a second before reaching for the loops. She stepped off, sur-rendering to the fall, letting herself plunge before she spread her arms and flew.

Bill had thrown himself after her and was close to her as she streaked above the cathedral roof, her feet inches from his face.

Arf followed, keeping higher, and they weaved at speed over the dark city. She drew a curving, twisting line to their road, fast and careless, and they hung, pan-ting, looking for danger below before they settled.

Nothing stirred, and they came down quietly and ex-pertly in the road. They murmured their good nights and separated at Jonk's gate. When her door closed behind her, Bill and Arf parted silently. They had done all they could and now exhaustion began to overtake them. They were clumsy at getting indoors, but it was the dead of night and nobody woke. They undressed and eased them-selves into bed.

Just once before they fell asleep they winced and looked into the darkness, aware of danger. But the night was still and they let their heads fall back. Before they drew their second breath they were asleep.

From the tip of the cathedral spire Jonk's scarf was pulled loose and fluttered down. Her glove followed it but caught on a little ledge halfway down and did not reach the roof with the scarf.

The scarf was still writhing in the air when a spindle-shanked figure, clinging to the gilded cockerel's back, un-hooked its leathery fingers and, with Elizabeth's black bag between its shoulders, flew off over the city.

14. The Tower

They slept late and woke to a grey, overcast day. The clouds hung low, sagging with snow. It was Christmas Eve but the excitement was like tinsel hung so sparsely they barely noticed it.

After breakfast they met in the road, still heavy-eyed.

'Anything happen?' asked Bill.

Jonk shook her head. 'I slept like a log.'

Bill had his shoulders hunched. 'I feel rotten,' he said.

Jonk was alarmed. 'Are you ill?'

Arf laughed. 'He gets like that,' he said. 'You don't have to pay much attention to him.'

Bill glowered but said nothing.

Jonk sighed. 'Everything looks so normal,' she said. 'No dog, no sign of leather men. You'd think they'd be keeping an eye on us.'

'I wish they were,' Bill grumbled.

'Speak for yourself,' said Arf. 'Enough has happened to me today already.'

They turned towards him quickly.

'What do you mean?' Bill made it sound like an accusation.

'Nothing to worry about,' said Arf, but Bill, glowering at him, sensed something Arf would rather now hide and kept at him until he told them.

Arf reddened slightly. 'When I crept in last night,' he said, 'I forgot to turn the mains switch on again and they thought the power cut was still on this morning.'

Bill started to laugh. It was rare for Arf to make a mistake.

'What happened?' he asked.

'Nothing much. I switched it on again.'

There was more to it than that.

'Tell us how,' said Bill.

Jonk saw the devil in Bill's grin and for once came to Arf's aid.

'Leave him alone,' she said. 'He's embarrassed.'

'Come on, Arf,' said Bill. 'Tell us.'

'My father almost caught me doing it, that's all. I heard them grumbling in their room when I got up and I crept downstairs in my pyjamas to put the switch on. I'd just done it when my father came down.'

'What did you do?'

'I stayed in the cupboard till he'd gone, of course.'

'A long time?'

'Quite long.'

'Was it cold?'

'Yes it was.'

'Poor old Arf.' Bill was amused.

'Leave him alone,' said Jonk.

Arf was indignant with Bill. 'I got so frozen,' he said, 'I was still shivering at breakfast time and I nearly spilt my tea.'

There was more to come. Bill straightened his face and asked, 'Didn't they notice?'

Arf's words came in an angry rush. 'Yes they did! My

father said to my mother, "There's something wrong with that boy, Edith." '

A mistake. He had said too much. Bill and Jonk leant against each other and laughed until they were weak.

Arf frowned and looked away.

'Arf,' said Jonk, gasping, 'we're sorry really.'

Her sympathy was so rare she almost coaxed a smile out of him.

'I suppose it was funny,' he said, 'but it was so cold standing there in the dark.'

'In the dark?' said Bill and almost choked.

Arf managed to keep his smile.

The morning dragged on. Bill was more restless than the others and by dinner time he had made up his mind.

'I'm going up to the city this afternoon to see what I can find out,' he said.

Jonk agreed. He would be able to get some things they needed in case they were called out that night. She said she would stay at home, not going outside alone, and Bill and Arf set out with what money they had been able to scrape together.

The first snowflakes fell as they left home, and the muffled shoppers who crowded the pavements were sprinkled with white on their heads and shoulders.

'People seem quiet,' said Bill, 'just as though they are waiting for something to happen.'

'It's Christmas tomorrow, don't forget,' said Arf.

'Perhaps that's it.' But Bill continued to feel that the lull was more than the usual one that comes when preparations are almost complete.

They caught a glimpse of the cathedral spire in the distance. The weathercock was tiny.

'Nobody could guess what's inside that,' said Bill. He thought of the cold night. 'It's difficult to believe we were up there.'

They did not stand looking at it for long in case they were being observed, but the city seemed to hold no danger unless it was the dull oppressiveness that seemed to slow even the traffic and make all the pedestrians sluggish.

They soon finished what they had set out to do, buying a torch, some batteries and three pairs of goggles because one of the most uncomfortable things about flying was the way the cold air made their eyes water. Then they stood by a shop window wondering what to do next. Bill ran a hand through his hair and shuffled his feet. Arf waited to hear what was on his mind.

'Tell you what,' said Bill, 'let's try and find the war-lord's palace or castle or whatever it is.'

'You mad?'

'Don't think so. I just think we ought to take a look where we were last night before it gets dark. His head-quarters must be around there somewhere.'

'A quick look,' said Arf. 'No more.'

They had often been to the old streets near the river and knew the quickest way there. Once clear of the crowds they broke into a trot, blinking the snow from their eyes as they ran.

They found the street where they had dived on the leather men.

'We certainly flattened them,' said Bill.

But there was no trace of them now.

The road was white, striped with black lines where an occasional car or lorry had driven along, but the street was deserted. In this area there were more workshops and junkyards than houses.

'Miserable dump,' said Bill.

'They're pulling it all down,' said Arf.

Half the buildings were boarded up. Where the boards were gone the windows were smashed.

Bill turned his head from side to side, sniffing. 'There must be something,' he said. 'Something we can see.' Suddenly he thought of a likely place.

'Scrapeshins Passage,' he said. 'Let's go and have a look down there.'

They walked until they came to a tall building that had been part warehouse and part offices but was now empty. It had a gaunt, plain front, the bottom floor split by what appeared to be a tall arched doorway in the centre. But it was not a door, it was the entrance to Scrapeshins Passage. It tunnelled right through the building and opened into a maze of lanes behind.

They approached from the other side of the road.

'I don't fancy it,' said Arf.

'You don't have to worry,' said Bill. 'It's blocked up.'

They could see into the mouth of the passage. It had been boarded up at the far end.

'Let's go across anyway,' said Bill.

The tunnel was gloomy and dirty. They picked their way through the rubbish and put their faces close to some gaps in the boards.

'Funny,' said Arf.

'What?'

'The street lamp is still burning on the other side.'

A flame was dancing through the broken mantle of a gas lamp on a bracket on the wall opposite.

'I expect they just forgot to disconnect it,' said Bill, 'and it lights itself every night.'

'Or it might be to help the police. I shouldn't think anybody is supposed to go down there now.'

Under the lamp the passage divided and they could see no more than a few yards of worn flagstones and brick walls.

'Let's go round the block and see what's on the other side,' said Bill.

They came out into the street again and went uphill towards a busier road that cut across it. They turned the corner and continued climbing until, quite suddenly, the buildings to the right of them ended.

'I never knew it was like that!' said Bill, for they were standing at the edge of a huge area of cleared ground that stretched away from them down to the distant river. Whole streets had been torn down. There were heaps of rubble that had not yet been levelled, but the snow had smoothed the landscape right to the edge of the demolitions. Bulldozers, parked for Christmas, were standing sheeted down against the walls they would be eating into in the New Year.

Arf pointed. 'Scrapeshins Passage must have come out somewhere there,' he said.

'Doesn't seem much point in exploring it; there's not a lot left,' said Bill.

The snow was thick enough to cake underfoot. Behind

them the traffic hissed and grumbled, and in front of them the landscape was desolate and dead.

'No palace here,' said Arf.

'Unless that's it,' said Bill.

A tall warehouse, standing alone where everything around it had been demolished, was the only building between them and the river.

'Ha!' said Arf.

Bill shrugged. Everything had gone stale. 'Shan't forget this Christmas Eve in a hurry,' he said.

They had found no palace and nothing had happened, and when they got home and talked to Jonk, standing at her back door, she had nothing to tell them. There had been no sign of Elizabeth.

'Come in out of that snow,' her mother called and they went into the kitchen. The house was warm and there was a smell of cooking. Jonk's mother was finishing off the Christmas preparations. They stood awkwardly, not knowing what to say.

'More secrets?' she said. 'Don't worry, I'm going.'

When she went out of the room Bill gave Jonk the goggles they had bought for her. She was wearing a dress and slippers. It was strange to hand her something that looked so sinister.

'See you tonight?' he said.

'Who knows?' said Jonk. 'I can't understand it. I've been hanging about all day, ready to do anything Elizabeth asked me, and not a thing has happened.'

'It will,' said Bill, 'before long. This can't go on for ever.'

All Jonk's certainty had left her. 'I don't know,' she said. 'I feel that something has gone wrong.'

They told her about their search for the palace and the cleared area they had discovered by the river, but this also was useless information.

'The whole city feels dead,' said Bill.

Jonk sighed. 'What a Christmas Eve!' she said.

Bill and Arf went home. All three tried to interest themselves in the preparations everyone was making for the next day, but their thoughts were outside where the snow was thickening as though to seal them in and prevent them taking part in great events that were about to take place elsewhere.

15. Night Call

A soft thud. Jonk's eyes opened wide in the darkness. She was not sure she had heard anything. She lifted her head from the pillow listening for her parents moving about downstairs. There was no sound. The air on her cheeks and nose was very cold. She reached under her pillow for her watch and looked at the green, faintly glowing hands. Two o'clock – she had been a long time asleep.

There was a bang on the window and she jumped. Then she thrust the bedclothes off and pulled the curtains aside. A flattened snowball was still sliding down the glass. In the garden below, a dark figure was standing on the white lawn.

Her fingers were trembling as she undid the window catch. The window was stiff and she heaved at it. It slid up suddenly with a squeal that was partly muffled by the snow that had piled thickly against it. The wind billowed the curtains behind her and snowflakes blew into the room. She leant out, her hands deep in the snow on the sill.

'Elizabeth, is that you?'

The face below was a pale blur.

'Can you come down?' It was Elizabeth's voice.

'Yes.'

Jonk pulled her head in. But as she did so a square

patch of light lit up the snow beside Elizabeth. Jonk lunged forward again, the wind snaking her hair and speckling it with snowflakes. The light was on in her parents' room, and Elizabeth was moving backwards away from it. But there was a worse threat.

'Look out!'

Jonk's shout made Elizabeth turn. One of the trees at the bottom of the garden seemed to step out of place. A leather man was running from the shadows, high-stepping across the snow, moving quickly.

Elizabeth, her thin coat floating around her like a cloak, faced him. He towered over her, long arms jerking forward. Her hand slashed the air in front of him. He bent double like a broken branch. Before he fell, Elizabeth had spun round and was running back to the house. She was right beneath Jonk, out of sight of her parents' room. Jonk could see the shadow of her mother or father looking out.

A gust of wind swept round the house and shook the bare branches of the trees. Elizabeth's voice was just loud enough to be heard.

'I shall be in the market place. Come soon!'

Then she was gone, moving along the side of the house like a hunting cat. As though the wind had shaken it loose, another leather man came from the trees. Jonk's window came down with a thud. She could hear footsteps on the landing. She plunged into bed, shaking. She felt snow against her face, and thrust her head under the sheets as her mother came into the room.

She heard her walk softly to the side of the bed and

begin to turn back the sheet. Jonk started up as though she had been suddenly wakened.

'What is it?'

Her mother's hand came up to stroke Jonk's head but she avoided it.

'What is it?' she repeated.

'It's all right, dear. I think you must have called out in your sleep.'

Enough light was coming in from the landing for Jonk to see a sprinkling of snow on the carpet. Her mother began to tuck in the sheets.

'I'm all right, Mum,' she said.

'Warm enough, dear?'

'Yes thanks.' Jonk pretended to yawn.

Her mother went out, closing the door quietly. They would think that what they had heard was the wind blowing round the house. The light under her door went out, and Jonk got out of bed shivering. She pulled the curtain back. Snowflakes streaked by close to the window and at first it was difficult to see beyond the glass. Then the clouds thinned across the face of the moon and she could see the garden. It was empty.

Jonk pulled on her clothes. Two pairs of socks, her gym shoes, trousers, windcheater and a scarf tied round her head. She put her goggles on over her scarf, put her arms through the loops of the little black bag, and last of all pulled on her gloves.

She eased the window up. The wind pressed against her. Quickly, she pushed the snow from the sill and climbed out. The sill was slippery. She crouched on it, holding to the window-frame as she pushed it down. The last inch was difficult but she managed it. Carefully, bracing herself against the brickwork on either side of the window, she stood up. She leant against the pane as she fumbled behind her head for the loops. As she pulled them, the wind flattened her to the glass with such force she thought she was going to be pushed through.

Impossible to take off like that. She thought it out, then acted. In one movement she bent her elbows, bringing her hands close to her shoulders, spun round and jumped into the wind.

Arms wide. The wind took her and tossed her like a sheet of paper. She was over the roofs and rising. She brought her arms closer to her sides and, pointed into the air like an arrow, she hung almost stationary. The moonlight through the racing clouds dimmed and brightened, and at first she could not recognize her own house below. Then she saw it and counted down the row of rooftops until she came to Bill's.

The lower she sank the more difficult flying became. The turbulent air over the roof-tops tossed snow like the spume of breaking waves. She lurched down, aiming for Bill's window. She was level with the gutter when suddenly the undertow of the wind sucked her backwards, lifted her helplessly and threw her to one side.

She thudded full length, face down, in the soft snow on the roof. It began to slide. She went with it. Too late to launch herself and fly, she tried to hold herself still but her hands slid over the tiles. She went over the edge in a cascade, blinded, grabbing at anything. With a jerk that tore at her shoulders her hands hooked in the gutter and she was hanging.

Snow on her goggles half-blinded her but she saw Bill's window away to her left. Then the clouds were torn open and the full light of the moon glared down. Bill's face appeared behind the glass, and a moment later the window opened and he reached for her.

Hand over hand she swung towards him. He sat on the ledge with his legs inside the room and steadied her as she got her feet on the sill and let go of the gutter.

'I've been waiting for you,' he said into her ear. He was half-dressed.

'Time to go,' she said. 'Seen Elizabeth.'

'Quieter,' he said. 'My brothers.'

She stood and flew, lifting smoothly into a pause of the wind.

Bill's window closed. Inside, he listened. His brothers were breathing quietly. He dressed quickly and went downstairs.

Jonk lifted over the roof-tops and came down in the road. The snow was so deep it was difficult to see the edge of the pavement and there had been no traffic for the last hour to rut its surface. She stood still, searching for leather men and ready to soar in an instant, but all that moved in the street was dancing snow.

Arf's window was at the front. She copied Elizabeth and made a snowball. Twice she missed. She looked round. Bill stepped cautiously from the porch of his house and crossed towards her. His aim was better. Arf's curtains parted, his face peered out briefly and the curtains dropped back.

They opened the front garden gate, pushing it against the snow, and waited in his porch. Jonk told Bill what had happened and repeated it when the door opened and Arf joined them.

Arf nodded. 'Do we fly?' he said.

Snow sped by the porch, paused on the wind, spun suddenly and whirled upwards.

Bill nodded, then turned his head to Jonk to ask, 'Buckle first?'

'Yes,' she said. The time had come for the last act of the struggle.

They stepped out into the street. The snow was well above their ankles.

'Christmas Eve!' said Bill. The houses were all dark, white-capped, waiting.

There was no time to go to the park.

They pulled their goggles down over their eyes, bent their heads into the wind and tugged at the cords.

Jonk was the only one who had experienced the storm. She bit into the wind thinly, but Arf and Bill faced it too squarely, lifted before they were ready and were flung away from her. Arf, the lighter of the two, went high. Bill's legs hit telephone wires before he was the height of the houses. He felt a wire stretch tight and break and then he was above the roofs in the full force of the wind. He saw Jonk below shifting through the currents like a canoe fighting rapids and he streamlined himself to rock down beside her.

They were a few feet above the houses, gasping. He twisted his head from side to side, and then shouted, 'We've lost Arf!'

Jonk looked about her. Above was the roaring sky. Arf had disappeared into it.

'Keep above the street lights for a minute,' Bill yelled.
'He might be able to see us.'

They waited, silhouetting themselves against the
lighted snow, but Arf did not come.

'No use!' Jonk shouted. 'We'll have to go!'

Her head, goggled, did not look human. He wanted to
shout to her to wait, but he knew she was right.

Her voice came to him again. 'Keep close!'

The moon flared, cold and bright, and they rose like
two fish slipping through broken water. Then the air was
steadier, a huge river full of flying flecks that stuck to
them, whitening the heads and shoulders and loading
their arms so that they had to shake it off. They flew
across it, slicing sideways into it, dipping and lifting with
first one on top and then the other.

Gradually they fought their way across the city and
struggled upwards as they approached the cathedral. The
wind whistled at the spire's tip and the gaunt cockerel
breasted the gale in his private world above the city.
They came up on his leeward side slowly, elbows bent,
and clutched at him together. There was no snow on him.
The wind had wiped the metal clean.

They bent over the bird's back, clutching at whatever
gave a hold. Jonk reached down between the metal plates.

Arf, a speck in the sky, saw the whole city. He was too
high. Breathing was difficult. A swathe of snow blotted
out the pinprick pattern of lights. Swept along in the sea
of the sky, he almost panicked. Then the lights glimmered
again. He fixed his eyes on them. Strange how silent it
was. The sky should be howling. Then he realized what

151

caused the silence. He was being carried by the wind and in the depths of the sky there was nothing for it to roar against.

There was a thin smile on his face as, deliberately, he tilted forward, pointing his arms in a dive.

Jonk's face was her goggles and the black ring of her open mouth.

'It's gone!'

Bill held his glove in his teeth and reached inside his windcheater for his torch. The inside of the weathercock was empty.

A lull in the wind was broken by a hiss that had them crouching against a new danger. Arf plummeted past them, opened his arms slowly at the end of a dive that had seemed endless, curved up towards them and clung neatly to the spire just beneath their feet. He was white with frozen snow.

'The buckle's gone!' Jonk yelled.

Arf's white head nodded. He had no breath to speak.

Jonk clung to the edge of the bird. 'It couldn't have blown down,' she shouted. 'I fixed it too tightly.'

Bill put his torch away and got his glove on. For several seconds the three of them remained motionless, clustered at the top of the spire like carved figures. They knew there was only one thing to do.

'Ready?' said Bill.

Jonk nodded.

He looked down. 'Ready?' he called.

'Market place?' Arf's voice was small in the wind.

'Yes. Keep together!'

They dropped away one after the other, travelling with the wind, high and fast.

They had not far to go and the market place, empty even of parked cars, was easy to pick out. They were buffeted as they came in over the buildings but their skill was greater now and they dropped where they wanted to be in the centre of the square. It was sheltered by the buildings and trees and the wind was less rough. They released the cords and pushed their goggles up. As they brushed off the worst of the snow they examined the square. No sign of Elizabeth. The wind boomed overhead, but the square seemed quiet, snow-deadened. Nothing moved. They felt the cold for the first time, rubbed their arms and stamped their feet in the deep snow.

'Here!'

A voice called from the side of the square. Elizabeth was under a tree. They ran to her.

She seemed smaller than ever. A street lamp shining through the branches of the tree criss-crossed her face with shadows. Her eyes glittered like an animal's gazing from its lair. Her coat hung loose. Her feet, still in high-heeled shoes, were almost hidden in the snow. If she was cold, she did not shiver. She was like someone in great distress who had got beyond caring what she looked like or what became of her.

Jonk faced her. There was no greeting.

'We have not much time!' said Elizabeth. She held out her hand for the buckle.

Jonk hesitated, afraid to give the bad news.

Elizabeth's eyes went quickly from her to the others. She was nervous, and something angered her.

'Why aren't we under attack?' she said. 'Why is the square empty?'

'We haven't got it.' Jonk's face was twisted as though she was in pain.

The small, hard, glittering head lunged towards her like a snake's. No words. The eyes flickered, piercing Jonk's.

Jonk stood where she was and told what they had discovered. When she finished, Elizabeth drew her head back, her eyes dropped, and she stood quietly with her back to the tree.

At length she looked up.

'They stole the power of flying from me,' she said. 'Now one of them can fly. And worse, the strength of the belt grows; I can feel it.'

Jonk was sliding her arms from the loops of the little black bag. 'Take it,' she said.

Elizabeth's haggard face smiled.

'Useless to me now, my dear. The belt has a force over me that holds me to the earth.'

'But we fly.'

'Because they have the buckle, you are no longer a danger to them. They seek me, only me.'

'But we must be able to do something.'

'You have acted well,' said Elizabeth. 'You are not to blame that the belt is completed. But your part is finished. You must go home.'

She put her hand on Bill's arm, then Arf's and lastly held Jonk's hands in hers. Jonk felt the warmth and the hardness of the rings.

'What will you do?' said Jonk.

Elizabeth's smile was almost sad.

'I am going to get the belt.'

'You can't! He is too strong!'

'We shall see.'

'Let us go with you.'

'No. That is impossible.'

'We will go, nevertheless,' said Bill.

She stood back, still smiling. Her eyes held theirs. Nothing moved.

'Good-bye,' she said as though she intended they should leave.

They stayed where they were.

Suddenly the wind checked its course over the roof-tops, gathered itself and plunged into the square. Already full of snow, it ripped up more from the ground and advanced on them like a creature itself. It choked and blanketed them, spinning around them, pressing itself into their faces. They held their hands to their eyes but could see nothing through the white wall.

As suddenly as it had risen the wind dropped and the snow settled. They saw the trunk of the tree, but Elizabeth was gone.

16. Scrapeshins Passage

Jonk's footsteps crunched in the snow. She spoke two words quietly.

'Follow me!'

She beat her way into the sky and streaked off over the city. It was the dead of night. Street lights sparkled on the frosted snow. In sleeping bedrooms Christmas parcels lay waiting to be opened. The three flyers and a few torn whisps of cloud glamorized by the moon were the only moving things.

They had taken off too quickly to put on their goggles, and the tears forced from their eyes by the bitter air froze on their faces.

Jonk flew low, speeding towards the black area in the bend of the river. At the edge of it she checked and hovered. Below, easy to see against the whiteness, Elizabeth was walking in the street. They knew where she was going. She disappeared into Scrapeshins Passage. Instantly, Jonk dropped away.

'Wait!'

Bill's voice made her open her arms to hold the air. They edged over the building at a walking pace, waiting to see which path Elizabeth took when she came from the tunnel. There was a brief flicker of black under the gas lamp and she disappeared into the lane on the left.

In order not to come down too close to her they pitched over the roof-top and landed in the street. In the tunnel the boards were down. They crossed them, turned left under the lamp and trotted in single file along the narrow alley. It twisted and divided again. There was not enough light to see footprints. They pushed their scarves from their heads and listened. A foot crunched in snow away to their right.

Deeper and deeper into the maze. Black walls closed around them. Another tunnel. At the far end a figure moved against a bank of snow. They turned left again. The walls soared above them showing only a slit of sky.

They were close to her now. They heard her coat brush against a wall.

They turned right, going downhill in a cobbled alley where little snow had penetrated. The buildings were derelict, windows broken, doors hanging open, rubbish piled against the walls. The air was freezing but still smelt of decay.

They paused. They could neither see nor hear anything of Elizabeth. They went forward at a jogtrot. The alley ended in a blank wall. To the right a pair of tall wooden gates led into a yard. One of the gates had rotted and sloped back. They climbed through the gap. The yard had belonged to some sort of workshop and the snow only slightly softened the outlines of heaps of rusted metal. The building at the far side was roofless and stars showed through its empty windows. Something creaked inside it. They waited, half-crouching, their hands ready to grasp the cords.

Silence.

'Look!' Bill kept his voice low. He pointed. A line of footprints crossed the yard. They were still on the trail.

They crept forward. The footprints went through the empty doorway of the roofless building. They stepped inside into a corridor with bare floorboards. To the left an empty room; to the right another. Deeper into the building. The boards groaned under their feet. A room on their left had an empty doorway that looked out on to snow. They crossed it. The snow sparkled in a broad street.

The footprints continued outside, turning left and going downhill. The street was lined each side by a row of black terraced houses. Where they ended, chopped off by the demolition work, the road also ended. Beyond it was the bulldozed plain that stretched as far as the river. In the centre of the plain, its blank windows underlined in white, the solitary warehouse stood.

Elizabeth was near the end of the nearer terraced row, but the warehouse, as tall and narrow as a tower, drew Jonk's eyes.

'He's in the tower!'

They all knew what she knew. In the bend of the river the warlord had had his palace. He had come to reclaim it.

Elizabeth began to cross the open ground.

'Come on.' Bill stepped out.

They were like drawings in a book, black against white.

Half-way to the tower Elizabeth paused. She turned and looked back. They stepped quickly into an open door. Elizabeth moved on. Bill's foot was crossing the threshold as he began to follow when Jonk's hand on his arm pulled him back. She said nothing, but her grip was fierce. He turned, but his eyes did not reach her. He saw for the first time the inside of the house. It was in the middle of the row, a mean little house like all the others, and he should have been standing in its front room. But he was not.

They had stepped into an immense hall. For the entire length of the street the houses had been hollowed out. A double row of regularly spaced windows, and a row of open doorways stretched down each side for as far as they could see. Moonlight shone through in bright shafts that leant to the walls like buttresses, diminishing into the distance.

But Jonk saw more. Something rippled in the furthest moonbeam, then the next caught the movement and then the next. The base of each shaft came to life as though the floor was undulating towards them. The place was packed with leather men. This was their barracks.

Against Jonk's foot something black was stirring. Her cry bent blind heads towards them like grass in a gale.

Backwards. Slow-moving nightmare feet stumbled on the doorstep. Snow clogged their running. Fingers failed to grasp loops. The black doorway was writhing, reaching for them.

Arf, to one side, lifted. Bill followed. Jonk fell. Above her, against the depths of the sky, a polished dome, tilted, stooping. Bill spun and came like a sword blade through the air, slicing a swathe through the enemy, cracking thin ribs, crushing cold bodies. In the space he cleared round her she rose to her feet, spread her arms and flew. He, held by the foot, kicked with his full force and was free as Arf slashed at other reaching arms.

There was a roar as they jerked into the air. They saw the white of the open space blackening as leather men from all sides ran to circle the lonely figure of Elizabeth. She stood where she was, alone in a white circle of snow, waiting for the ring to tighten. The roar died and they heard the beat of their arms as they hovered.

The moon shone on the face of the tower. At its base a vast doorway gaped as though to devour the white ground. One leather man, one only, left the throng and ran, pricking the snow, into the shadow of the door.

A pause, and then he stepped out again. He held across his arms something that shone less bright than the snow but seemed the master of all light. The leather man raised it above his head. The belt hung as heavy as a pike's belly, and the head of it, the buckle, glinted with wickedness.

There should have been a roar. Instead, the movement of the leather men ceased as though they had been locked into place. They were as silent as frozen debris. Only Elizabeth moved. She ran to the edge of the circle. It broke in front of her and she was through.

Then, from the mouth of the doorway, the black dog ran. It was between her and the belt carrier, mane flattened, lips curled back. Three yards from her it leapt. Her hands came up. The jewels on her fingers shone like starlight. The dog twisted in the air, head back, legs sprawled as though to stop its leap and turn away. It went past her shoulder and pitched on the snow. It lay dead with snow in its mouth.

Elizabeth was beyond it, but the belt carrier had gone.

In front of her there was only the gaping door. And now the leather men had come to life, but she stopped, ignoring them. She and the warlord, still hidden, were doing battle.

The black horde approached and divided around her as though a wall of force kept them away. The three watchers felt the pain of the silent struggle. The gap between her and the leather men contracted and they closed in front of her. Then her power pushed them back and the door was before her again. She advanced a step and the leather men came with her. She moved slowly as though she was moving their entire weight.

The black doorway gaped and in face of it Elizabeth faltered. The power of the belt was proving too great. The horde pinched in again. She waved them back and opened a gap, but when she tried to walk she was held, pressed against an invisible wall. For the last time the leather men moved across.

It was Jonk who began the dive to rescue her. Like stones they dropped into the ring. There was no noise but the night seemed to scream. They felt pain. Their muscles ached. It was difficult to breathe. They stood back to back facing the writhing wall of leather men that strained to reach them but who were still held back.

Jonk spoke between her teeth, every word separate.

'Fly . . . with . . . us.'

Elizabeth looked only towards the doorway. Her face was pale, her eyes large.

'Go now,' she said. 'Dawn . . . the Green Man . . .'

The mention of the name brought her defeat, as she knew it would. The roar that engulfed them seemed almost to rob her of life. She sank to the ground. They tried to raise her, but she thrust them away.

'Go!' They saw the word on her lips but could not hear it.

They obeyed. The glitter of the rings was the last thing they saw as they lifted, then the black circle closed over her.

They watched the tower swallow the horde. They heard the doors thud shut. Then they flew away, thin, exhausted, wandering aimlessly over the quiet, frozen city.

They searched the sky above, but nothing followed them. They were left to roam because there was no danger remaining in them.

17. The Green Man

They flew without thinking, beating their arms slowly like rooks flying home at dusk. They crossed their own street, but it was like looking at a map – it was difficult to believe anybody lived there.

They flew until the streets petered out in a waste of snow. Even the trees were weighted with white as though they had been turned into marble.

'Dawn,' said Jonk. 'When is dawn?'

She lay stiffly in the air, like a statue resting on glass.

'Hours yet,' said Bill.

She seemed not to hear, and then her pale, smooth face turned towards him. He could not see her eyes but he knew they were blank, holding no expression.

'We must rest,' she said, and her voice was toneless.

Then, as though from a long way off, they heard Arf. 'Find a farm,' he said.

They searched for landmarks and discovered that, without a conscious thought, they had flown along the road to the backlands. Already they were half-way there.

They saw a farmyard and came low. The sinking moon printed their shadows sharply on the long roofs of the buildings grouped around the yard. In the gable end of one there was a door just under the roof, probably leading to a hayloft. They swept once round the silent, empty yard and, as the others held back, Bill went down and landed on the door sill. He tried the latch and the door swung open. In a moment all three were inside.

Below them, a horse stamped and snorted. They held their breath. The horse settled down rubbing its head against the side of its stall.

It was warm in the loft, or seemed so to them. They used their torches and saw piles of farm gear, tarpaulins and ropes, bins and bales of hay. They found a place to sit and a cat came up the steps from below and rubbed against them.

'Bring us luck, puss,' Jonk whispered.

They said little, sitting silently in the dry, musty dark. They would have said they were thinking of leather men, Elizabeth and the cold sky, but what was in their minds did not alter from one minute to another. They were not thinking, they were enduring time. Arf alone fidgeted, often shining his torch on his watch to convince himself during their long silences that he was where he was and not asleep and dreaming. Occasionally he went to the door and looked out at the bright stars, and the hours slid by.

At length Jonk went to the door and stood there for a long time.

When she stepped back she said, 'Get ready.'

They refastened their scarfs and settled their goggles in place.

'I hope you know what we're going to do,' said Arf.

Jonk nodded. She knew only one thing and that was enough – they had to be above the Green Man at dawn.

She took off first, standing on the door sill and stretching out her arms as she leant forward into a white world that was now cut by long black shadows. She floated out and lifted quickly above the buildings. Arf followed, and Bill, coming last, pulled the door shut in case carelessness should bring them bad luck.

There was the familiar sting of icy air in their throats as they climbed, and then they levelled off and flew swiftly. For a time Bill led, but he knew that it would be Jonk who would decide their final moves. Elizabeth seemed to act through her. He glanced at her goggled head only a few feet behind and above him. Her scarf was already white with frost. Arf, a step higher, rocked slightly as his arms thrust him on.

Below, the shadows extended and deepened, wrapping landmarks in a sooty blackness, but here and there a pin-prick of yellow light came from windows where somebody's Christmas Day had begun. The thought that at home his brothers may already be awake made Bill suddenly spurt forward. It was involuntary and he soon slowed and allowed the others to catch up.

The last lights fell behind and they were above the lonely lands where no tracks broke the surface of the snow, and the forest lay white and still.

They found Elizabeth's house. There was no sign that anything had been disturbed. They came lower, riding finger-tip to finger-tip, the hiss of their glide fading almost to silence as they paused above the house. The low hedges were lost under the snow, the outer wall of the garden dipped where it had been broken in one place but there were no footprints through the breach.

They left the house and beat quickly across the heath. The unbroken snow was dimpled with shadows, but a sudden band of darkness surprised Arf.

'Higher!' he called.

They pulled themselves up with him. Panting, they looked down. The smaller shadows had faded into the background. The bigger ones told them what lay below. A shape bulged under the snow, pushing it up like a monstrous figure under sheets. They shied away, not wanting to be directly above it.

They came together, their voices whispering above the hiss of their arms.

'No sign of anything moving,' said Bill.

'Still half an hour to dawn,' said Arf.

Jonk was searching the ground.

'Come with me,' she said, and dropped away.

They plummeted out of the sky, dropping in the spot she chose close to a clump of bushes and putting the forest between them and the Green Man. Their feet crunched through the snow's crust. Arf opened his mouth to speak but Jonk gestured at him to stay silent. She pushed her goggles up but in the pallid light reflected from the snow her eyes were hidden under her brows and her lips were black. Snow Maiden, thought Bill. She faced the trees that hid the Green Man. She did not move, and they stood motionless beside her as gradually the moon edged out of the sky and extinguished itself.

The night was soundless. The only movement came from the twinkling of the stars and the faint whisp of their breathing.

In the blackness before the first fringe of daylight crept

over the horizon behind them, Jonk removed her goggles and scarf, dropping them at her feet. Bill and Arf did the same, asking no questions.

A sudden savage stab with her arms and she was gone, streaking across the snow. An instant later they followed. They were either side of her and slightly behind when she began to climb over the trees. Above the heath she hung high, head bent like a kestrel's.

She saw the dot emerge, a speck of black from the shelter of the trees, and move like a fly along the leg of the Green Man.

The sky began to pale; a thin light emphasized the coldness of the earth. She waited. Bill shifted so that he was above her, as though to protect her.

Arf looked up. A star went out. Then another.

'Look out!' His shout and the rush of a plunging body came together. He had seen, too late, the leather man above them fold his arms and fall.

Bill took the full force between his shoulders. Arms and head jerked back like a shot bird. He cried out and fell, tangled with the spider bunched on his back.

Arf saw them go. They separated. One spread its arms; the other plunged on. Arf watched his friend fall, twisting in the air that no longer gave him grip. He disappeared and Arf was possessed by a fury that thinned him to the bone. Falling was not fast enough. He thrust himself downwards until the air screeched and he could not breathe.

The leather man lay lazily, peering after his victim. The shriek reached him too late. His arms jerked as he tried to slide clear. Arf brought up his knees and hit the black figure like a boulder.

Bill, falling, saw the sky but no earth. He tucked one arm and rolled into a dive. The trees were coming up quickly. Arms wide, head exposed, he slowly twisted his hands. They began to bite the air, but not enough. He was too low, falling too fast. He held his head back, his eyes almost closed, as the roof of the forest heaved up at him.

He came at it at a shallow angle, very fast. The topmost branches whipped him, stinging, then thicker ones ripped. He skidded along the forest top in a fountain of snow, crashing from tree-top to tree-top. Then suddenly the battering ceased. He lifted clear. Both shoes had gone from his feet, and one trouser leg was hanging in strips.

Jonk inched forward, covering the black spot that was moving over the chest of the Green Man.

Arf's fingers clawed leather. He dug deeper. The leather man writhed and thrashed and he was flung off. Both spread their arms and circled. The leather man saw Jonk hanging motionless above and climbed. Three swift strokes brought Arf within reach of a leg. He grabbed and held.

Bill saw the struggling figures and climbed. He lurched above them, reached swiftly to his belt and snatched the knife that had touched the buckle. Like a swimmer treading water, he waited, choosing his spot.

Jonk, clear of the struggle, saw the snow tremble.

Bill settled until his chest was almost touching the back of the leather man. The long arms rose and fell, flipper-like, straining against the weight of Arf, and a grating roar came from the smooth head. Bill could see the cords at the shoulders. He brought his arms forward and sank on to the leather back. With his left hand he found the cords; with the knife in his right he cut them. The roar from the head became a shriek but his own cry was louder.

'Let go!'

Arf swam clear.

A loose end of cord brushed Bill's face and whipped away, trailing from the leather man's hand. The other skinny arm came up, reaching, and clutched the cut cord. Bill dipped in a new attack but as the leather man's arms spread in the attitude of flying he saw no attack was needed. The leather man's arms flapped uselessly.

A roar came up from the falling figure, anger turning into fear. A pause of silence, a faint, distant scream, and then, just clear of the trees, the snow was pocked with a black dimple.

Bill and Arf lifted their heads to search for Jonk. They saw her and tried to climb to her, but their arms were sluggish. It was not only exhaustion after the fight; the cold evil of the leather man had worked on them as they clung to him. They were numb, almost helpless. They sank towards the ground.

From the head of the Green Man the snow slid. The black figure of the warlord stood on the dome of rising ground that lifted him tree height and paused. Tufted and shaggy, the enormous face below him rose as steep as a cliff, still unfeatured, but from its crevices it observed.

High in the sky, Jonk was caught in the first beam of the sun and burned golden. Below her, pale as moths in the shadows, Bill and Arf watched a shoulder of earth lift and heard the suffocated thud as the snow fell from it.

A crack appeared the length of a leg and part of the white roof of the forest fell in where a foot stirred. Trees tilted, but the cracking of the timber was swallowed in the rending of the earth as the great body tore itself out, and a field of snow slid from chest to thighs in a roaring wave. Not yet at full height, crouching still, the Green Man loomed over the forest. The ripped earth lay behind him like his shadow in the snow.

They gazed up at Jonk, a little flake of gold deep in the sky. She did not move. As yet in the shadow of the earth, unseen by the sun, the Green Man rose. From his fingers a whole tree curved down, its roots still solid with earth.

Bill and Arf stood in the snow. The head rose above them. It was marked with gullies, a faint face. Sheep could have grazed in the hollows of its eyes.

Jonk moved then. They saw her spiral down no bigger than a firefly.

The great head of the Green Man swayed below her. The figure of the warlord was in the middle, stock still, his triumphant ride to the city about to begin. Her eyes searched beyond the head. The ground was bare; no hordes of leather men. She would face their master alone. The fight was for the belt. That was all she knew.

She stooped like a hawk, falling faster and faster until the wind flattened her cheeks and pulled at the corners of her eyes. And then the head of the Green Man tilted back and he was looking at her from the huge sad pits of his eyes and his hand was rising to take her. She slid sideways, missing her aim. The hand came up swiftly as earth lifted by an explosion. She slewed further sideways. The grass-backed fingers reached. One scythed by with a roar. She was sucked after it, something struck her leg and she was sent spinning.

She dug her fingers into the air, kicked for fear of being caught, and found herself rising. Earth and sky were confused and then she saw she was close to the Green Man, skimming his chest. His head tilted above her, looking down, and both hands came up to gather her from behind. She flew up, daring the face. Shaggy chin, deep gulf of a mouth, broad hill of a nose and caverns of eyes flicked by. Then she was skimming the green grass of his brow, climbing to the warlord.

She streaked into the attack as the dome lunged up. She hit the grass hard. She felt a flash of pain, darkness engulfed her, and she rolled limply to the warlord's feet.

She fought to open her eyes, struggling out of the darkness, her chest heaving. She saw him standing over her and she hit out.

Her hand struck stone. The cloak of the warlord was stone. Legs and arms were hidden in folds of stone above which a head of stone gazed from blank eyes at the horizon, but the belt was there, wedged in the stone folds, glinting above her. She was on her knees in front of it, clutching the grass, bewildered. She had seen him moving and now he was a statue, rooted to the head of the Green Man like a bloodsucker, a vampire.

Suddenly she knew what had happened and knew that her task was more terrible than she could have believed. The warlord had occupied the Green Man; the Green Man had been entered and must obey.

She got to her feet as the great hands came seeking her. The buckle was level with her eyes. The golden snakes circled the man-shape in the buckle and the man was upside down. She reached for it as the blind fingers advanced, grass brushing grass.

She hooked her fingers behind the metal and pulled, The belt, cleft in stone, did not budge, but the warlord in the Green Man felt her touch and set the great hands in motion. She tugged, twisting. The huge fingers furrowed the dome, ploughing towards her, and still she held on.

As the earth pushed up under her feet she leapt clear. The statue rocked. It tilted and in that instant she saw her only hope.

Deliberately, she curved downwards, fluttering past the face of the Green Man. She was gasping and flew awkwardly, easy to catch. He reached. She slid further away. The hands came after her. She tumbled lower. The Green Man stooped. She touched the ground. Bill and Arf watched the hands arch over her.

The dank smell of the earth was in her nostrils when Jonk felt the cords vibrate and suddenly her hands were forced together and made to move in a swift little jerking motion she knew well. Elizabeth was aiding her for the third time.

Pillars of earth surrounded her, closing in. A gap a yard wide remained. She shot through it and arched upwards with the speed of an arrow. Her target was the statue. It leant forward on the Green Man's head. The swift path of her flight took her in a tight curve above it and she brought her weight down on its back.

It lurched. She rose and plunged again. The statue tilted further. But the warlord knew his danger and the head of the Green Man jerked to bring the stone upright.

The move was too sudden. The statue's base was wrenched from the earth and it toppled forward.

The warlord cried out then through the lungs of the Green Man. The mouth of the head opened and from it rolled and echoed a boom of despair. The Green Man rose full height and the warlord within him made his hands reach for the statue and the belt. It was too late. The statue slid forward, face down, over the Green Man's brow. From the jagged socket it left behind, Jonk saw something move swiftly to be absorbed in the statue. The statue lost its stiffness and she dropped on it, feet first, thrusting it headlong down the slope.

Jonk lifted. The warlord slid down the face of the Green Man, the belt still around him, but now it was useless to him for he was falling head first and the buckle was brought upright.

And the Green Man became himself. His hands plucked the enemy from his face and lifted him by the feet, held him dangling against the pink dawn and shook him.

Jonk, climbing, heard the crack as metal snapped and saw the belt flung free. She curved easily into its path and caught it as the Green Man let his foe fall. The warlord spun, thudded into the Green Man's face, lay still for a moment and then, lifelessly, slid over the edge of the trench that was the Green Man's mouth and disappeared. The mouth closed.

The Green Man looked up towards the tiny figure of Jonk high in the sky. Then the caverns of his eyes closed and the landscape of his face became gentle.

From below, Bill and Arf saw the tower of earth give up its life. It began to collapse, a huge structure from which all strength had gone. The lowest parts subsided in rumbling landslips. Next, thud followed thud as earth masses thundered down, and the ground throbbed with their weight. Then, from the greatest height, chest and head came down, streaming loose earth like plumes of black smoke.

The ground bounced under the Green Man. As trees laid themselves beside him, Bill and Arf were tossed by the ground wave and fell sprawling in the snow.

They raised their heads to see a white mist of crystals still hanging over the crumbled body, and seconds later the thunderclap of its collapse was still wandering in the distance.

'Hey! Hey! Hey!'

A tiny voice called from the top of the sky.

Standing on snow streaked with black powder dashes of earth, they watched Jonk float down.

18. Christmas Day

Ten feet above ground she let go of the loops, and dropped. They ran to her. She held the belt out to Bill.

'Here you are,' she said. 'Wear it!'

He took it and buckled it round his waist.

'Ah!' said Jonk. 'It looks fine.'

The snow where they stood was dusted with earth, and black and white mingled in the long broken slope of the Green Man's body. They stood where they were, letting their eyes take it in, saying nothing. A great door seemed to have slammed shut. Bill put his hand to the buckle and the other two looked at him.

Jonk drew in her breath sharply. 'Your leg!' she said. 'It's bleeding!'

Bill glanced down. One leg showed bare where his trousers were ripped from thigh to ankle and it was marked with blood. He noticed for the first time that his feet also were bare and bleeding. He was making pink footprints in the snow.

He started to laugh. Jonk looked from him to Arf. Behind his glasses Arf's eyes were closed and he was wheezing. For a moment she did not realize it was laughter and her frightened eyes darted back to Bill.

'We've done it!' he roared.

She put a hand out to touch him but midway she was caught by their laughter and bent double

They staggered and laughed, sat down in the snow and laughed, hugged each other and danced. And when Arf said 'Merry Christmas' they clung together and ached.

And then as suddenly as their laughter had started, it ended. The same thought was in their minds.

'Elizabeth!' said Jonk.

They tugged at their cords together. Extra anxiety made Bill frown as he remembered the numbness that had forced him and Arf to earth, but now they rose as swiftly as Jonk. They did not look back but flew straight towards the edge of the sun that now showed over the horizon. Never more than tree height, they streaked towards the city, the hiss of their flight waking many a light sleeper as they beat over the villages and farmhouses, not caring if they were seen.

The fields flashed by, then the outskirts of the city where the street lights were paling to yellow. The streets were deserted but lights were on behind many curtains and smoke was rising from chimneys.

They skimmed over Scrapeshins. Everything was made neat by the snow. The tower was dark against the dawn. They came down near its foot, hovering just clear of the ground. In the trampled snow lay the dog, savage jaw still wide open.

They touched down and walked to the door. It was shut fast.

'The windows,' said Bill.

Like bees at a honeycomb they flew to every window,

calling for Elizabeth. Every floor was empty. No leather men. Nothing.

Next they searched for footprints leading away from the tower, but all they found were those between it and the half-demolished streets. They searched the long hall of hollowed-out houses but it was deserted.

Dejected, they stood in the snow. Only Arf dared say what was on their minds.

'I don't suppose we shall ever see her again,' he said.

Jonk was near tears. She could say nothing.

Suddenly Bill stamped his bare foot in the snow.

'But she's not dead!' he said. 'She can't be dead!'

'How can you know that?' said Arf.

But Jonk turned her eyes on Bill, eager for him to dash her fears.

'If she was,' said Bill, 'do you think we would be able to fly?'

It was true the little bags kept their power in spite of Elizabeth's wishes, for even a leather man could use them, but surely if she was dead they would become useless. Jonk knew Bill was right. They had beaten Elizabeth's enemy and she was alive somewhere.

They flew to prove it to themselves, lifting from the deserted plain until they were higher than the tower that had been Elizabeth's prison, and still higher until they dwindled to tiny points. They saw the earth below like the page of a book. The city was cupped in the hollow of their county, and away to the east the sea touched the white land with white fingers. Jonk's confidence came back.

'She found us once before,' she said. 'She'll find us again.'

She yawned. Her eyes watered with tiredness. They breathed the high air deeply for the last time and began the long, slow spiral down.

'Sleep,' said Jonk. 'We need sleep.'

But it was not until they were almost home that they thought of their empty beds. Their disappearance must have been discovered. If so, they had a victory to talk about, but talking was not what they wanted. They parted over the road and dropped homewards.

Bill's bruised bare feet kicked the snow from the window-ledge. He eased the window open and squeezed into a house that was still silent, still breathing as softly as it had all night.

Elizabeth was sitting on his bed.

He stood in front of her. The room was grey with a light that seemed no light at all.

She smiled but he could not smile. He could see nothing but her face. It absorbed him. Sometimes it seemed huge, gazing down at him, forcing him down, and he was afraid. Then it seemed to shrink until it was no bigger than the pupil of his eye and still he could see every detail.

'Now you may take it off.'

The sound of her voice brought the details of the room into his vision. His brothers lay fast asleep. He realized he had been swaying, on the point of collapsing. He put his hands to the buckle and unfastened the belt. He handed it to her and she took it smiling.

'Tell the others,' she said.

He nodded.

She stood up. He was afraid at first to meet her eye, but when he did so he saw there was nothing to fear.

'Go to bed,' she said.

Suddenly he was flooded with happiness and wanted to talk, but she shook her head. He stood and watched her cross to the door. She smiled at him once more and was gone. He listened, but the house was utterly silent.

He undressed, rolling his torn trousers into a ball and putting them under the bed. He would dispose of them later, or think of an explanation. His cuts and scratches did not seem too bad. His feet were tingling and warm on the carpet.

'White as snow,' he mumbled, looking down at them.

He lay down. Christmas morning. He wondered if there were parcels at the foot of his bed and lifted his head. There were several. He let his head fall back on his pillow and slept.

The others did not see her, not even Jonk, but windows and doors opened easily for them as they entered their houses, and nobody woke.

The day crept slowly into their rooms, lingering as though to let them sleep, and it was late for a Christmas morning before any of them awoke. Even then they were awake, before the rest of their households, and their first thought was to break the news about the Green Man to everybody, but as they were on the verge of getting out of bed, they each, even Arf, had second thoughts. It suddenly seemed too much trouble; the explanations would take a great deal of time, and what proof did they have to show but a dead dog and a mound of earth? Also, deep within themselves, was a desire to keep it all secret.

They rested content for a moment, but then the need to tell everything, particularly flying, grew strong again. To fly again on Christmas morning would overshadow any present they might get. Just for the sake of being able to do that they would tell everybody their story. They felt under their pillows for the black bags. They were gone.

Arf's mind was made up in an instant. There was an explanation for all that had happened and he was not going to say anything until he knew it. He set about starting his Christmas Day.

Jonk smiled and hugged her pillow. There was no need to do a thing now but enjoy herself.

Bill searched every fold of his bed for the bag and found nothing. No more flying. He lay back staring at the ceiling and touching the scratches made on his legs by the topmost branches of the snow-covered forest. Often during the day he felt them smart, and the memory of flying came back like a dream he had not wanted to end.

It was a perfect day. After the dangers, the normal excitements of Christmas were something less and they experienced them with a calmness that increased their pleasure. The secret stayed with them.

19. The Reward

Arf smiled and smiled. It seemed to Bill the smile had not left his face the whole of the winter, and he had smiled all spring, and in summer he was still smiling.

'Hallucinations,' said Arf. 'We got into a bit of a state and imagined the whole thing.'

'What about those torn trousers and the cuts on my legs?' said Bill. 'You can't explain them away.'

'You were worse than the rest of us because it was your idea, and if you had to go charging around in the snow by yourself on Christmas Eve, what can you expect?'

Bill, standing facing Arf in the garden, seemed about to hit him.

'Oh don't bother with him,' said Jonk. 'You know you'll never convince him. He's got that sort of mind.'

Bill swung his head towards her.

'Don't glower at me,' she said. 'I know it all happened.'

'Ha!' said Arf.

'Proof!' said Bill. 'I'll get him proof if it's the last thing I do. I've showed him the broken glass in the museum, he saw the tower before they pulled it down, and he even came out once to the Green Man, but no, he has some dull, stupid explanation for everything.'

'Not dull, scientific,' said Arf.

'I'm going,' said Jonk.

She knew exactly how the frustrating argument would go. The one thing she did not understand was how they could bear to go through it all again.

She left Arf's garden and went out to sit on the front garden wall. In the end Bill would join her.

The day was so hot the tar on the pavements had softened, and tiny fragments of crushed stone glittered in the road surface. Just like frost, she thought. She half-closed her eyes. The sun was hot on her face and arms.

'Run and ask that boy friend of yours if he can give me a light.'

She opened her eyes. Elizabeth Goodenough stood in front of her. The same spiky fringe. Eyes as blue as the sky.

'I've been busy,' said Elizabeth. Her smile wrinkled the corners of her eyes. 'Did you think I would never come?'

'I always knew you would,' said Jonk. She was calm. She knew this was the last time they would meet, and did not want to ruin it.

They looked at each other. Elizabeth's smile did not fade.

'The belt has been made safe,' she said, 'but it has meant a great labour for me, greater even than when it was first broken.'

She did not explain what it was that had absorbed all her energy for seven months, and Jonk did not ask. There were signs in the little woman of great exhaustion, but there was also satisfaction.

'It's time for your reward,' said Elizabeth.

'I don't want one.'

Elizabeth nodded. 'But you must have it. Patterns, remember? Things must be fitted into place, and a reward is one of them.'

Jonk's gaze was steady. She did not reply.

'You will find it where everything began,' said Elizabeth. 'Now run and fetch that boy. I want a light.'

She opened her handbag and took out a cigarette case as Jonk stood up. Before she turned into the gateway, Jonk paused.

'Good-bye,' she said.

Elizabeth's smile faded.

'Good-bye,' she said.

Bill and Arf ran out ahead of Jonk, but Elizabeth was not where Jonk had left her. She was standing at the end of the road. She waved. They ran towards her, but the little woman turned suddenly on her high heels and disappeared round the corner. They ran after her, but when they reached the corner she was gone.

'She can't be far,' said Arf. 'Come on!'

He began to run, but Jonk and Bill stayed where they were.

'No use?' said Bill.

Jonk shook her head.

'Blast it!' he said. 'I wanted to fly again. Is there any chance?'

'No,' said Jonk.

'What did she come for then? It couldn't have been for nothing.'

'I'll tell you when Arf comes back.' She needed time to control the tears that brimmed her eyes.

'Look at that fool Arf,' said Bill. 'He'll never find anything.' He turned towards her. 'Just like Christmas again,' he said, 'but there's no need for her to run away now, is there?'

Jonk shook her head, not looking at him. Bill fell silent, then he said, 'We won't see her again, will we?'

Arf came up. He was hot and he was angry.

'You saw her,' he said. 'Why didn't you come?'

Hallucinations. The taunt was on Bill's lips but he did not say it. Jonk wiped her eyes with her fingers and smiled at Arf.

'It *was* Elizabeth,' she said. 'You weren't mistaken.'

'Well why . . .?'

'Because she had already told me all she had to say. We've got to go to the backlands.'

'Have we?' said Bill. His face brightened. 'Why?'

'To complete the pattern. That's what she said.'

'Well I'm not wasting any money going out there,' said Arf.

He was still arguing when they got on the bus, but the summer smell of the countryside coming through the open windows, and the green and yellow fields eased his temper.

'All snow last time we were here,' he said. It was not strictly true; they had been to the backlands once since then.

Jonk was silent and Bill said little. It was not the fields or the colour of them that affected him so much, it was that the air was so different. In winter it had been empty, now it was full of moving things, not only birds, but insects and seeds. There was always something glittering. He longed to fly.

They found the track. It was sandy and dry.

'The forest doesn't look so black,' said Bill.

'Because we know there's nothing to be afraid of,' said Arf. 'Probably never was.'

But among the trees the air was heavy and the silence made them hurry. They made for Elizabeth's house. There was a gap in the trees and an overgrown patch of sand.

'Is this the place?' said Bill. 'Are you sure?'

'Yes,' said Jonk. 'Look, you can still see the pattern.'

Among the grass and ferns, bushes ran in ragged rows.

Bill turned to Arf. 'Convinced?' he said.

'Of what? There's nothing magic in a few tatty bushes.'

'But there was a house here.'

'Houses can be pulled down.'

'All right then; the Green Man.'

Heat shimmered over the heath. A long, irregular bank of grass lay where the Green Man had fallen.

'And that,' said Arf, 'has been there for centuries.'

The evidence was on his side. There was no broken earth, the grass grew evenly on the slopes, and butterflies flitted around bushes that could hardly have been disturbed since they rooted. They climbed to the top.

'This is his chest,' said Jonk. She stopped.

'Anything wrong?' asked Bill.

She laughed. 'Nothing. I just thought I felt the ground move.'

Arf rolled his eyes upwards. 'Oh, not again!' he said.

'Dear old Green Man,' said Jonk. 'I liked him really.'

She looked around her. The heath was flat and peaceful. Nothing to fear, yet she had a feeling they were being watched.

Other mounds were scattered nearby and they thought they could trace the Green Man's arms and legs. The mound they were on ended in a rounded hillock.

'I want to have a look at his face,' she said.

She ran ahead and clambered up the little hill. Behind her they were arguing.

'See those trees,' said Bill. 'Over there, flat on the ground. I reckon that's where his hand pulled them up.'

'A gale did that!' said Arf.

There was a hollow where the Green Man's mouth had been. Jonk walked round it to his eyes. They were no more than depressions in the ground, smooth and grassy. At the bottom of one rainwater made a shallow pool that flashed in the sun. It was too lifelike. She did not want to go closer. And then what Elizabeth had said came back to her. Patterns. Magic patterns had to be completed.

She went down into the hollow and looked in the water. It was a circular pool and very shallow, reflecting the blue of the sky like an eye's iris. She looked for the pupil and there was one – a golden disc in the centre, under the surface. She reached in and lifted it out. It was their reward.

Bill and Arf came down into the hollow and found her sitting with it in her lap. It was a golden dish, two feet across with figures embossed on it, men and horses fighting.

They knew they were not meant to keep it. They took

it to the museum, and there their reward became something strange and almost impersonal because other people shared in it. The curator was excited, even became a little friendly and before the week was out an archaeologist, an eminent man, came from London and went with them to the Green Man and they showed him where the dish was found.

He was a grey-haired, well-fleshed man, a bit like a more prosperous Mr Roberts. He had the same hooked nose and seemed to enjoy lonely places.

'Odd,' he said, looking into the hollow. He filled a pipe and lit it before going down. 'Not a sign of subsidence,' he said. 'Earth's quite firm. Are you sure you found it here?'

'Yes,' said Jonk. 'Just under the water.'

'Well, the water's gone now. Not a crack in the ground. It must have been exposed long ago, and nobody noticed it. Well, well, well.'

They took a liking to him, and he to them. He let them follow the dig which, because of the danger that other objects might be close to the surface, began immediately. He brought in a team of helpers and day after day they went out in the archaeologists' cars to the caravans and tents that had sprung up around the Green Man.

The Green Man, they were told, was a tumulus that because of its irregular shape had not before been recognized and had got on to no maps. Bill risked saying that the mounds were somewhat man-shaped, and one day he mentioned the theory of the Green Man. He was taken seriously. 'Very plausible,' said the archaeologist, and the theory was discussed at length.

And Jonk, who had found the dish, caused another stir. She heard some of the diggers discussing where the chieftain who was certain to be buried in the tumulus was likely to be found. She pointed to the Green Man's mouth.

'Try there,' she said.

They smiled, but they remembered what she had said when later they dug at the spot and found a skeleton, mangled and disjointed.

'Badly damaged,' said the archaeologist. 'Most interesting. He hardly seems to have been buried with reverence.'

'Hardly,' Jonk agreed.

But this discovery did not excite the encampment half so much as what they found when they dug into the Green Man's chest. Hardened almost to rock were the ribs of an ancient boat.

Over and over again the archaeologist said 'Extraordinary! A ship burial all these miles from the sea! And what is more remarkable and entirely unique is that the ship has been turned upside down!'

Arf was impressed, but Jonk and Bill exchanged glances, and then Jonk spoke.

'Listen,' she said.

The archaeologist paused and everybody else stopped speaking. She blushed, but from under her eyelashes she saw Bill nod and she raised her head, pointed, and said, 'Under those ribs you will find a heart of gold!'

The main treasure was piled neatly just where she said.

THE FINDING
Nina Bawden

Alex doesn't know his birthday because he was found abandoned next to Cleopatra's Needle, so instead of a birthday he celebrates his Finding. After inheriting an unexpected fortune, Alex's life suddenly becomes very exciting indeed.

RACSO AND THE RATS OF NIMH
Jane Leslie Conly

When fieldmouse Timothy Frisby rescues young Racso, the city rat, from drowning it's the beginning of a friendship and an adventure. The two are caught up in the struggle of the Rats of NIMH to save their home from destruction. A powerful sequel to MRS FRISBY AND THE RATS OF NIMH.

NICOBOBINUS
Terry Jones

Nicobobinus and his friend, Rosie, find themselves in all sorts of intriguing adventures when they set out to find the Land of the Dragons long ago. Stunningly illustrated by Michael Foreman.

FRYING AS USUAL
Joan Lingard

When Mr Francetti breaks his leg it looks as if his fish restaurant will have to close so Toni, Rosita and Paula decide to keep things going.

DRIFT
William Mayne

A thrilling adventure of a young boy and an Indian girl, stranded on a frozen floating island in the North American wilderness.

THE SONG OF PENTECOST
W J Corbett
Pentecost is the leader of a tribe of harvest mice who have to go on a perilous journey from their polluted wasteland home to a new place to settle in the hills. A marvellously witty and exciting adventure story with intrepid heroes and deceptively charming villains.

JOE AND THE GLADIATOR
Catherine Cookson
How do you manage to look after a horse if you've no home or money? This is Joe's problem.

THE WIND IN THE WILLOWS
Kenneth Grahame
The classic story of the riverbank adventures of Mole, Water Rat, Badger and Toad now freshly interpreted by one of England's finest contemporary illustrators, John Burningham.

JET, A GIFT TO THE FAMILY
Geoffrey Kilner
Who would have believed that a tiny, spindly, jet-black puppy was to lead the Reynolds family into the exciting world of greyhound racing? This perceptive and entertaining novel is about how Jet turns out to be a truly exceptional dog.